ABOUT THIS BOOK

He came for his mate. She can't fathom the idea of it. But the gods' will always wins.

Chevy Walker didn't come to Havenwood Falls to spread his wings or find a safe haven. No, he followed his natural instinct and the scent of his mate. He's got the bloodline, the power, and the money to make men and women fall at his feet, so why can't he bring one willful woman to heel? Chevy can play the nice guy. He hasn't broken the rules once—but even nice guys have their limits.

Hannah likes men, but not well enough to give up her freedom. Not like her ancestor, River, who had her power locked away in an amulet by a dusty old vampire. Hannah has her life in order and control of the heat and flames. She might not know the origins of her power, but she knows her future, and it does not include a cocky, controlling stranger—no matter that his voice gives her chills or how delicious he smells.

But Chevy's lineage could be the key to filling in the blank spaces in Hannah's history. She can choose to accept him as her mate willingly, or she can allow the madness to consume her until there's nothing left of either of them but a spark. For that seems to be the will of the gods.

HAVENWOOD FALLS SIN & SILK BOOKS

Taming the Beast by Nadirah Foxx

Plans Laid Bare by JD Nelson

Shift of Fate by Victoria Escobar

Stolen Wishes by Victoria Flynn

Damned Allure by Justine Winter

Savage Salvation by Kristie Cook

Dark Seduction by Michele G. Miller & R.K. Ryals

Soul Laid Bare by JD Nelson

Stray With Me by E.J. Fechenda

Chase the Flames by Desiree Lafawn

Flirting With Death by Nadirah Foxx

Also try the signature line, Havenwood Falls, the historical paranormal line, Legends of Havenwood Falls, and stories from the local supernatural college in Sun & Moon Academy.

Stay up to date at www.HavenwoodFalls.com

ALSO BY DESIREE LAFAWN

CONTEMPORARY ROMANCE

The Permanence of Pain

Beck the Halls – A Gallery B Christmas

Glass City Hearts

Gabe (Book One)

Dino (Book Two)

Jesse (Book Three)

PARANORMAL ROMANCE

Kiss the Ashes (A Legends of Havenwood Falls Novella)

Havenwood Falls Short Story Anthology 2018

Shiny Dancer: Mountain Mermaids (Sapphire Lake)

Lost to the Deep: Mountain Mermaids (Sapphire Lake)

CHASE THE FLAMES

A HAVENWOOD FALLS SIN & SILK NOVELLA

DESIREE LAFAWN

This book is dedicated to every fan who reads Havenwood Falls, whether you've read one book or all of them. It's your dedication and love for this series that allows us to come together and continue to create new stories in this fabulous world. Thank you for loving us.

CHAPTER 1

CHEVY

I'd never witnessed a bar fight before. As someone in my position, I've had my share of struggles. I've fought for power, position, and authority. I've fought for my freedom in an oppressive establishment, but I'd never even seen a bar fight. Until now.

I'd also never seen a woman that small throw a punch hard enough to knock a guy twice her size clean off his feet. He went from towering over her as she sat in a chair, talking quietly with her young, curlyhaired companion, to flying through the air about eight feet away. It happened so fast, I might have missed the entire exchange if I hadn't already been staring at her. For reasons unrelated to her fight.

If the caterpillar from *Alice in Wonderland* reincarnated as a hippy, I was surely looking right at him. I'd been in Havenwood Falls for two days, and while the owner of the Haven Saloon wasn't the weirdest person I'd met so far, he certainly was one of the most interesting. Bent Brent—I couldn't get a read on him. Human for sure, but there was no way he didn't know that half his clientele was of the supernatural variety. Not when he had a shelf behind the bar, so low I almost couldn't see it, of bottles with labels that didn't have a damn thing to do with human consumption.

It couldn't be just the circle of smoke that wafted around his head that made him so mellow he didn't blink at the shocking violence happening right in front of him. That home roll clamped between his teeth might have been a special blend, but there wasn't a sticky on this earth that could make a man that relaxed. No, Bent Brent had the laid-back air of a man who had *seen some things*.

He didn't even quirk an eyebrow at the five-foot-nothing redhead who just sent a six-foot two-hundred-fifty-pound meat pinwheel somersaulting across the bar.

"You probably want to move over a hair." I barely heard the words as the barkeep mumbled them around the smoke still tucked between his lips.

The big guy landed right next to me, and if I'd been any slower, I would have taken a boot to the kneecaps as he sprawled haphazardly on his back, legs folded up against the bar wall and one arm flung over his face.

"Damnit, Hannah I wasn't ready." For a man who just had his innards reorganized, he sure had record recovery time. He was already on his feet and lumbering back to the table before I had time to blink.

"I wasn't aware there was a time frame I was supposed to operate in." The voice rang out merrily from across the room. Light, and maybe just the tiniest bit musical, if I wanted to admit my bias. "You said take my best shot. I took it." She walked toward where the man stood, mere feet from me, and patted the bigger man on the arm as she passed him. He flinched, but grinned good-naturedly.

"You're too little to hit so hard."

"I work out." She smiled back at him and laughed, making her way to my side of the room.

She reached the bar then, and the beast inside me, the one I shared my soul with, raised his head and eyed her hungrily. She was the one we were looking for. The one we came all the way here to find. This slip of a woman with fiery orange anime hair and a mean right hook was my mate.

I'd been following the pull for a few hundred miles. I would know her anywhere. That's the power of the mate bond. Genetics. Or at least that was what I'd found out, after a lifetime of thinking it was just heresy.

The mate bond existed, and every lie the elders of my caste had told me fell at our feet. They raised us to think we weren't like other shifters. No, our lineage was special; our sacred blood fragile. The elders paired us off to make sure we did everything in our power to perpetuate the continuation of our species.

At least that was the doctrine.

But I knew the truth now. And someday the rest of them would too, but before I could blow the conspiracy of the elders of my kind wide open, I had to come back with proof. Ranting like a lunatic and railing against the system about the medication we took to "stabilize our fragile blood and moody beasts" would not convince anyone to stop taking the meds. No. I had to find and bring them proof, and the only way to do that was to make an example out of myself. The only way to do that was to leave the family.

If it weren't for my best friend Baz, next in line for an elder position, I never would have made it. But here I was, clean from a lifetime of suppression drugs and feeling the pull of the mate bond for the first time in my life. It dragged me all the way across several states and up a mountainside. A feeling so strong I couldn't ignore it —neither could my beast. Dreams of smoke and ashes plagued me every night, but not nightmares. No, these dreams were filled with scents and sounds so pleasing I thought I would go crazy trying to find their source.

And then at the bottom of the mountain I'd caught her scent. The scent of my mate.

There was one for me, and she was right there in front of me. Everything I'd suffered in my thirty-some years of existence had led me right to this point. The lies, the grand plan, the breaking away to find out the truth—it all led up to this moment.

She was perfect.

"BB, can I get a . . ." Her words trailed off, and it was in that moment I knew. I didn't even have to see her sniff the air to tell the exact second she caught my scent. I wondered what I smelled like to her? I knew what she smelled like to me. Burning wood. Campfire. Fall leaves.

Sex.

That was there too, the underlying intent. When two mates found each other, the result could be explosive at first, as the desire to connect became overpowering. At least that's what I'd read. I'd been suppressed by the system of lies I was raised in, so I didn't have much time to process the information. But my rock-hard response had me believing that small bit of lore I'd uncovered before I'd made the move. Before I'd started my hunt.

I needed to touch her.

I also needed to not be a creep about it.

"What smells so good?" I didn't know who she was asking, but she was looking right at me, the dark pupils in her amber eyes expanding and contracting. Target acquired; I was in her sights. "Hello." She licked her lips, and my blood sang in response.

I'd done all of the research I could do with the limited resources available, but every bit of information I found pointed to how overwhelming and absolute the instant attraction and pull would be. I was prepared to exert iron control over my emotions and physical desires while I navigated the treacherous path of my mission. It didn't occur to me she would be just as affected as I was.

She touched my arm and I knew I would follow her anywhere.

"I'm Hannah. You're new here. What's your name? Where are you staying?" Those amber eyes studied me, and a light flickered there, a candle burning, nothing more.

That was a lot of questions to answer for someone who wasn't even looking me in the eye. I wondered if she expected my dick to answer, because her gaze moved down to my zipper and stuck there. If she didn't knock it off, I would give her something to look at, all right.

"I'm Chevy Walker, I'm from Arizona, and I'm staying at Whisper Falls Inn." Was she at the bar with anyone? Would she introduce me to them? What was her next move? Her hand was still on my arm, and I swear I could feel her heartbeat through her fingers and the fabric of my shirt—through the air even.

"The inn? That's close. Walking-distance close. That's good. Let's go there." And she turned toward the door, her hand still on my arm, steering me toward the exit with no other option but to follow her. Because I *had* to follow her. I inhaled her scent deep into my lungs and imprinted her on my body. The beast inside me did the same. This whole trip—this whole mission—was for her. It couldn't be this easy.

But it was that easy.

No one followed us out of the bar. No one raised an eyebrow at either of us as we left. I'd only been in Havenwood Falls for two days, and barring the sweet old ladies I met on my way into town, it seemed like a real *mind your own damn business* type of place.

But even a place where everyone minded their own probably wouldn't look the other way regarding two people boning in the street. Which is what *almost happened.* As soon as the old-fashioned batwing bar doors closed behind us, she was on me, hands grabbing, lips teasing. She went for my ear first, and I barely had time to catch her before she crawled up my body and stayed there, legs wrapped around my waist.

She weighed nothing.

She felt amazing.

For someone so slim and lithe, her curves were as soft as I thought they would be, and her small teeth nibbling on my earlobe froze the breath in my lungs. I had to lock my legs to keep from stumbling. The urgent need to possess her punched through me; I'd felt nothing so strong in my life. The books did not cover this kind of need. If I didn't strengthen my willpower, I would nail her in the street, and by the sounds coming out of her throat and the way her fingers dug into the flesh of my arms, Hannah would accept it willingly. The only other option was to hurry—or come in my pants like a first-timer.

I didn't have the heart or the willpower to push her away from me, so I did the next best thing I could think of. "Can you run?"

She grinned like a lunatic.

Turns out, she could.

There was no one at the inn, not in the hallways and not working the desk. Or at least it seemed that way as we escaped to the room, but most likely we were too wrapped up in each other to notice any innocent bystanders. I don't even remember taking the stairs, but I remember the sound of her small gasping breaths. Would she make the same sounds as we mated? I couldn't wait to find out. We made it, after an eternity of keeping our hands to ourselves, and I shut the door to the suite I rented, the lock clicking in place with a sinful finality.

Finally. I could touch her. Peel back the layers of clothing and savor with touch and taste the skin laid bare. There wasn't a spot of visible flesh I didn't want to bite, and some I couldn't see that I wanted to put my mouth on.

I don't know why I thought I would be in control.

She went straight for my pants. And by went straight for them, I mean she ripped them right down the seam on one side and tore them off. Hannah was *strong*, and a lesser man would have been terrified at the ferocity with which she disrobed me.

But I was not a lesser man, and there was nothing about Hannah I couldn't handle.

I appreciated her little gasp of happy surprise though, when she saw I went commando. Underwear was too restricting, and the less I had to remove before shifting the better. But she didn't know that. She knew none of it yet.

She will. My beast huffed in agreement.

"Hannah, slow down."

Her busy hands stopped briefly, and she uttered a small grunt of impatience. "Why?"

Why? I didn't know why. I couldn't shake off the lust-filled haze long enough to think of a single good reason she shouldn't do exactly what she wanted to me. But while I was fumbling for the words for what I was feeling, she dropped to her knees and slid her warm, moist mouth over the tip of my cock, stopping time completely.

"Hannah. Stop." I was as firm as possible, which was difficult with her mouth wrapped around my shaft and her hand cupping my balls. "Woman. Please."

Her only answer was to close her mouth and swallow, the muscles of her throat working to send me to the brink of destruction. In the space of a few mind-blowing seconds of pleasure, I realized two things: Hannah was a woman used to doing whatever she wanted whenever she wanted, as was obvious by her refusal to get off her knees and spit out my dick; and I was so turned on by the thought of taming her, I almost let her get away with it.

But I couldn't. Establishing dominance early was important for me and my beast. It was our nature to be alpha, and giving up the reins of control during sex was not acceptable—at least not the first time. Once we got to know our mate a little better, there would be plenty of time for experimenting, but right now she needed to stop or I was going to come, and Hannah would have made the first power move. Reaching down, I fisted my hands in her wild hair and tugged—not hard enough to sting, just enough to get her attention.

"Hannah, stop." I repeated my earlier order.

I don't know if she planned on obeying, but I broke her concentration enough for her to let go of me, and I hauled her back to her feet, spinning us both around, and pressing her back against the door so hard, she gasped with pleasure.

Oh? So Hannah likes to be handled a little bit. I squirreled the information away for future enjoyment.

"I'm the alpha here." I emphasized my point by gripping her hands and holding them above her head, my other hand resting lightly against her throat.

"Oh yes." The words were the barest of whispers. I bet she didn't even know she said them.

"I'm going to fuck you, Hannah, and you're going to look me in the eye while I do it." The scent of her arousal intensified—my filthy words pleased her. She wiggled against me but I didn't pull away— didn't allow her an inch of room. There was no way she didn't want me to pin her down, not with her eyes closed and that peaceful fucking smile on her face. Screw it. I'd held back for long enough. There was no one here to see or interrupt us. The beast inside me demanded I finish what the mate bond started. She was right there; no need to wait any longer. Hannah reared back against my restraining hands not because she didn't want me touching her, but because she wanted to hang on to that role of being in control.

Not today. Not right now. She had to submit; my beast wouldn't allow anything else. We were just animals, after all.

"Tell me what you want me to do to you, Hannah. Tell me every dirty thing going on in that mind, right now." Still holding her hands immobile, I blazed a wet trail with my tongue from her ear to her collarbone, pausing at intervals to suck the flesh of her neck, bringing the blood to the surface. Leaving hickeys was juvenile. Maybe. But I would mark her as mine for anyone to see and to hell with the consequences. She was *my* mate. *Mine.* She wriggled, and I bit her firmly on the shoulder, wrangling a shriek of pleasure from her lips.

Hannah liked it rough. Excellent.

"Say it." I ground the words out in frustration. *Tell me what you want, Hannah. Give me control.* She wrapped her legs around my waist and used the weight of me pinning her to the door to grind her pelvis against mine. She still had her jeans on and whimpered at the extra barrier between us. I wanted it gone too, but she still hadn't given me what I wanted.

"Do you want me to stop?" She'd better not fucking say yes.

Eyes wild with a burning light, she shook her head, wrestling with getting what she wanted and giving up control. Later I would let her climb me like a tree. I would let her have her wild way with me. But this time, it had to be on my terms.

She needed to say the words. Accept me. *Submit.*

She brought her face to mine hard. Punishing. Teeth clashing against teeth as she bared them even while kissing me. I still held her pressed against the door, and the more she struggled, the more my cock swelled and the tighter she locked her legs around my waist, grinding against me, desperate for relief. The sharp tang of blood entered my mouth. It could have been mine or hers at this point, and I didn't care. She may not have wanted to give up control, but Hannah wanted this—wanted me.

I felt the moment she decided.

"Take me." The words were murmured so low, I wondered if I'd heard them at all—then louder. "Be rough. I—I can take it. I want it." I grinned to show my approval, and she smiled back at me, her anger at being topped bleeding into the passion of letting go. "Break me, Chevy." She issued the challenge with a feminine growl.

Fucking finally.

"Keep your hands up," I ordered, and she obeyed, leaving her hands above her head with the palms facing out. I had my own strengths. I could have ripped her pants off of her just as she'd done mine, and she probably would have liked it—but I didn't. Instead I sank to my knees on the floor in front of her, maintaining eye contact the entire way down. It might have been a submissive position, but I was in control. Even as I slid her zipper down agonizingly slowly and pulled the denim over the flare of her hips even slower, I was still in the position of power.

Hannah's panties were blue lace and barely there, her need evident by the darkening of the fabric where her arousal soaked through. I could rip those apart too—even thought about it briefly —but I surprised her by spreading her soft thighs apart with my hands, as far as I could while her jeans still trapped her ankles in place and buried my face in that wet scrap of lace, inhaling deeply. A strangled cry erupted from her throat, but I didn't give her time to react. Running my tongue along the wet fabric, I sucked her protruding clit into my mouth, right through the lace.

Her thighs clamped around my ears, and the hands I'd demanded stay above her head dropped to my hair, pressing me even closer to her. I sucked harder, and she screamed.

"Oh God. Chevy, *oh God.*"

She did not understand how right she was.

CHAPTER 2

HANNAH

I envy people who can blame their actions on drinking and crawl underneath a good hangover to avoid the world for a while. As a supernatural being, I don't get to do that. Booze doesn't affect me like it does most people, and I drink beer because I like the bubbles, not because I can get drunk. And I'm not about to drink the liquid hallucinogens Bent Brent has lining his bottom shelves. Nope, I could do keg stands for days and accomplish nothing but an intense urge to pee and a case of the burps.

So when I opened my eyes at the butt crack of dawn feeling refreshed, invigorated, and just so damned good I couldn't explain it, I remembered every bit of what went down the night before. Every. Single. Thing. Including who belonged to the arm slung around my middle, over the blanket I recognized by the pattern as belonging to Whisper Falls Inn. Where I had spent the night having rowdy, very *hot* sex with a stranger whose name I barely knew.

Chevy.

Oh, I could tell myself I didn't remember his name, but my mind wouldn't let me lie to myself. Chevy Walker, holy shit. I'd never had a one-nighter so hot in my entire life—and I should know one-nighters—it was kind of my calling card.

I'm not promiscuous, and I don't sleep around, but I also don't date townies, so if I want to have any fun at all, tourists are usually my choice. Out-of-towners don't stay, they don't remember my name, and they don't shackle me with stupid relationship nonsense, which is just how I like it. Chevy Walker wasn't from Havenwood Falls, which meant he would probably leave soon, so that fit the profile for me. *Now how do I get out of here without waking him up?*

Gently. That was the first milestone. I needed to extricate myself from his embrace without waking him up. A stab of guilt surprised me, and I froze mid-wiggle. I normally didn't feel bad about waking up and jetting. I had nothing to be ashamed of, and Chevy and I made no promises to one another last night. So why was I feeling bad about leaving before he woke up? Did I want him to stop me?

Hell no.

Maybe it was because of the sex. That had to be it. Sex with Chevy was a living, breathing thing, something I couldn't compare to any previous experiences. That was why my body was reluctant to slide out from under the covers. That was why my heart was screaming at me to turn around and *look at him*, but my mind refused to accommodate. I grabbed my clothes from the twisted pile on the floor and slid my jeans over my hips, zipping them as fast as I could without making a noise. I shoved my feet into my boots, not even bothering to look for my socks, which were probably twisted up in the covers of the bed I refused to look at again. I put on my bra and jammed my arms into the sleeves of my button-down shirt without making a sound. I was almost home free. Seconds away from saying goodbye to the most mind-blowing sex I'd ever experienced. Seconds away from escaping any awkward morning-after experience that might occur. I just needed to turn the knob, leave, and not look back. I could remember last night in my dreams. And maybe sometimes in the shower, if the radio was on or Dade wasn't home. *God,* Chevy was fine. Last night was amazing, and I probably wouldn't go to hell just for turning around and taking a little peek.

A sleeping Chevy Walker was a work of art.

I shouldn't have turned around. As soon as I laid eyes on that dark hair, tousled against the pure white of the pillowcase, I was lost. Should a human being be so beautiful? I sniffed the air before I could catch myself—such a weird habit I'd picked up since yesterday. Then again, I'd never met a person who smelled like fresh baked goods before. I couldn't nail it down. Was it chocolate? Honey? Cookies?

Whatever it was, he smelled damn good, and I wanted to eat him. Had I said he was a beautiful human? No way was he human. He had to be . . . something else. Nothing dangerous though, unless you counted death by sexy thoughts. Because I was having those.

Sexy thoughts.

My arms, calves, and thighs were still sore from last night. My body moved on its own, and the next thing I knew, I was miles away from the door and standing next to the bed, my gaze raking over his sleeping form like I didn't just get my fill of him the night before.

It's okay to look for just a second more. He's sleeping. He'll never know.

One dark arm rested on the comforter, flattening the space I'd just wiggled out from. His skin was darker than mine, but not by a lot. I could thank my great-great-grandmother River and our First Nations heritage for my coloring. At least my tan skin. My hair was a separate matter. I wondered where Chevy got his coloring from. Was it even my business to wonder? I shouldn't care, but I wanted to know more about Chevy. I wanted to know everything.

Dangerous.

Every part of the body that peeked out from under the covers was dangerous. For making me want to look at it longer. For making me want to touch him again. For making me think any other thoughts beyond getting out of that room and going home, back to my normal routine. Back to my normal life.

But I couldn't stop looking.

Because that strong dark arm that had been wrapped around me all night was also attached to a thick, sturdy body. And that body had bent me in ways that a less durable girl would have difficulty recovering from. I wonder if he knew I wasn't human. Not that it mattered. No one could tell by looking.

His face was all angles and clean lines, and a light dusting of dark stubble decorated his chin, with those soft full lips arcing up in a smile, even while he slept. The angle of his nose complemented the high lines of his cheekbones, and my fingers curled up into fists to keep from reaching out and touching his face.

And those eyes. That deep brown stare that threatened to swallow me whole. I remembered how he'd looked at me in the bar last night. Like a man starving, and I was his next meal.

Kind of how he was looking at me now, except for instead of sexually charged, he looked sexually sleepy. If that was a thing. If it wasn't a thing, it should be, because my bones turned to mush as those thick dark lashes fluttered up and the corners of those drowsy eyes crinkled. His full lips followed suit.

"Morning."

Shit. Shit. Shit.

I was supposed to be out the door, not hovering over the bed drooling over a sleeping man like a deviant.

"I have to go now." *Great job, dumbass. Good with the making of the words.* I took a few steps back, closer to the door. I absolutely was not running away. I had places I needed to be. Work. I needed to go to work.

"Okay."

The word meant acceptance, but the tone of his voice smacked of other things. Darker things. Things I would probably think about later when I was alone. But not now. Right now, I needed to go or I would break every personal rule I had and throw myself back onto his naked body. He sat up in the bed as if waiting for me to do just that, the sheet falling from his bare chest to pool in a tantalizing puddle at his waist.

Shit. Two more steps backward and my palm touched the cool metal of the doorknob. One twist and I was home free. *Breathe, Hannah. It shouldn't be this hard.* My chest was tight, and my breath was coming in gasps. My heartbeat blasted a cadence in my ears.

Thump thump. *Don't go.* Thump thump. *Stay.*

"What are you?" The words were barely audible. I don't even know why I said them. There was nothing wrong with Chevy. He was a normal guy. I was the one on the verge of a panic attack over trying to sneak out of a hotel room. What the hell was wrong with me?

Chevy smiled again—a soft, sleepy smile.

"Hannah." Even his saying my name was like a caress on my skin.

"What?" And if my voice shook when I answered, what of it? I was anemic. Low blood sugar. I probably needed some orange juice or something.

"I'll see you later."

"Sure." *Not likely.* And with that parting word, I found my courage and the strength to turn the doorknob. I was out the door quickly, but not before I heard his laughter, like warm rain falling down around my ears. I shut it out when I shut the door, turning and running down the hall. Third floor. Of course he had a private suite on the third floor of the inn. The good thing about being at the inn was the location—right across the street from my shop and my upstairs apartment. The bad thing about being on the third floor was all the ground I had to cover trying to avoid running into anyone I knew.

I made it to the first floor before I ran into Michaela Petran, innkeeper of Whisper Falls Inn and general all-around nice girl. I didn't have a problem with her on any other day, but today I just wanted to go without talking to anyone. There was something wrong with me. It had something to do with Chevy, but until I was under my roof and putting some space between us, I didn't want to stop and make idle conversation with anyone.

I didn't care about gossip. I just felt . . . weird.

She stood there staring at me, her long dark hair pulled into a ponytail hanging over one shoulder and her gray-green eyes wide with surprise. Michaela was younger than I was, but in terms of responsibility she had me beat, having to raise her teenage siblings and take over the inn all before she was even twenty-five years old.

The only responsibility I had was taking care of my brother, Dade. And he was closer to my age anyway, so we mostly just took care of each other. Oh—and my glass shop, but that was my pride and joy and couldn't ever be a burden.

"Don't say anything." I didn't need a lecture, or her asking me questions I couldn't answer. Like why I was sneaking down the stairs like a fugitive.

"But—"

I cut her off before she could continue. "Look, I'm tired, and I just want to go home. Can you just act like you didn't see me right now? Please? I'll owe you a favor?" I wanted to get out of there so bad. What if Chevy came out of his room? What if he followed me? Would I be able to pull away from him again? I shuddered at the thought. If he were to walk down those stairs right now, I would probably jump his bones again, right in front of Michaela, and anyone else with the misfortune to walk out of their room at the wrong time.

I turned away from her and made a beeline for the front door. The one I could see from my apartment. The one that was just a few steps away. Just a few steps to freedom. Once I was outside, I could clear my head. I could get the scent of Chevy out of my mind and off my clothes. I could put enough distance between the two of us to just think clearly and I could . . .

"Hannah." Michaela interrupted my inner monologue and put her hand on my shoulder, shaking it gently. She chewed her bottom lip a little before finding the words she wanted to say. "I don't care what you were doing last night, although I had a couple of noise complaints down at the service desk from your . . . enthusiastic performance. I'm just saying, unless you are trying a racy new fashion, which I don't think you are, you might want to button your shirt up before you walk out the door."

Ah, shit. Shit. Shit. Michaela was right—my shirt was wide open down the front, my lime-green bralette winking at the world in the dim morning light streaming through the inn's windows. Gathering the edges of my shirt and my shattered pride together, I hastily shoved the buttons through the holes and cleared my throat.

"Thanks."

"Don't mention it." She didn't wait for me to say anything else, just kept going in the direction she had originally been headed, which was most likely around the corner to the office area.

She'd said *don't mention it.*

Believe me, I wouldn't.

CHAPTER 3

CHEVY

I let her leave this morning. I didn't want to, but I wasn't so far gone yet that I couldn't use my brain. Hannah was skittish, and who wouldn't be? If she was feeling even a fraction of what I was feeling of the mate bond, then she was probably scared out of her mind. Last night the lust had hit her like a tidal wave. I watched as it washed over her at the bar. I saw the exact moment her pupils dilated and her nose twitched.

"What smells so good?" she'd asked, but no one could answer. To everyone else in the place, it smelled like too many bodies, spilled beer, and expensive weed.

To her, it smelled like something else.

Like mate.

I knew, because I smelled mate too, but my mate smell was probably different to her than hers was to me. That's kind of how it worked. The scent was deeply personal, and difficult to describe. Not even the sensitive nose of a wolf shifter could pick up the smell; mate scent could only be smelled by the intended. It was biology. Well, the biology of our kind, anyway.

And Hannah was my kind.

Well, not exactly.

I felt the words rather than heard them as the beast inside me ruffled his feathers at the thought. *Quiet, you elitist.* The reprimand I gave was silent, and as always, ignored. I wasn't angry, though, not at him. How could I be? He was the other part of me, the beast inside. And most importantly, he was right. Hannah was not a shifter. And even if she was, she wasn't a shifter *like me.* There were so few of my kind in existence, we were truly a dying breed. But she was my kind's mate, and as such, per our biology, she was a child of a God. As were others of my kind. We stood on an entirely different level as a species. Somehow, somewhere in her heritage, a deity passed through her bloodline. It was a badge of honor.

Not all children of deities were mates. But all mates were children of deities.

Funny how the world worked.

I almost felt sorry for Hannah. She didn't know anything about mates, while I'd followed the pull of her for hundreds of miles. I'd searched for her. *I'd hunted her down.* She was my prey, and now that I'd found her, I would never let her go.

She thought she was free when she left my room at Whisper Falls Inn this morning.

Run all you want, little rabbit. I already have you.

"Dude, why the creepy smile?" Someone broke my inward train of thought, and I blinked as the face of the one who'd spoken slowly came into focus. Addie . . . Beaumont was her name? A nice enough looking young girl, if I were in the market for such things. Which I wasn't. My Hannah was everything—she just didn't know it yet. My skin itched to be near her again, and it had only been a couple of hours since she'd left my bed. My body reacted negatively to her absence, but I was prepared. And it wasn't that bad, which meant she hadn't gone far.

"So, have you found her yet?" Addie wasn't even looking at me anymore as she bent over my arm, laid on the table with my wrist facing up. She was focused on her work, which today was putting the tattoo on my body that allowed me temporary residence inside the wards of Havenwood Falls. Every visitor had to register with the powers that be, in this case the Court. Funny thing was, I didn't find Addie—she found me. She'd knocked on the door, introduced herself, and pretty much told me what was up.

Direct and honest. My favorite personality trait.

"I did." She asked me what I was doing in Havenwood Falls, and I told her. Finding my mate.

"And how did it go?"

"About as well as it could for first meetings, I guess." I wasn't hedging. I was being as honest as I could, given the circumstances. I wasn't going to tell someone I'd just met all about my love life. I'd say what I needed to say and that was all. Addie rubbed a cleansing wipe on my skin and, with gloved hands, tapped a little bottle on its end. It was clear there was nothing in the bottle, but she acted as if she was pouring something out into a smaller cup on the table next to where my arm rested.

Noticing my skeptical look, Addie smiled. "Just because you can't see it doesn't mean it isn't there. Come on, as a shifter you should know this."

"Touché."

It was nice not having to hide who I was and have a conversation about it like it was no big deal. Where I came from, there were more shifters like me, but we still had to be careful talking about that side of ourselves in mixed company. The human-to-shifter ratio for my caste was a lot more skewed in Arizona than it was in Havenwood Falls. And we didn't have the protection of wards, a coven, or any kind of barriers. We governed ourselves.

"How long do you think you'll be in town?" She paused when I didn't answer right away. "Look, it's just a question just like any of the other ones you already answered. It's part of my job, but it's not an interrogation. I have no reason to think you are here for any reason other than you mentioned. Although I would be lying if I said I wasn't interested in your business. Shifter mate relationships are insane. I mean, I have seen some shit."

"Well, I don't actually know. I still have responsibilities at home I need to deal with, and Hannah seems a little difficult."

"Hannah?" Addie's hand stilled, and her head snapped up so her eyes could meet mine. "Hannah Pederson?"

"I didn't catch her last name. Is there more than one Hannah?"

"She's the only one that counts. Short, crazy orange hair, dresses and acts like a man?"

I didn't agree with her last point, but it was clear we were talking about the same person. "Yeah, that's her. What's the problem?"

"Not a problem," she said, drawing the word *problem* out until it was four syllables long instead of just two. "Hannah is just headstrong. Doesn't like authority. Kind of a rebel, if you want to think of it that way." She never looked up as she spoke, just continued running her tattoo gun over the lines on my skin, her needle buzzing low, completing its task. It wasn't a complicated design; it didn't have to be. The tattoo was temporary, a talisman that marked me as a legal visitor to Havenwood Falls.

And it let the so-called Court of the Sun and the Moon keep an eye on me, according to Addie. They were apparently the end-all and be-all around here.

It was fine. I wasn't concerned about any higher power worrying about my motives. Apparently, times had been troubling recently, and there was cause to be extra suspicious of visitors, especially supernatural visitors. I didn't care. I had nothing to hide in a town full of supernaturals. Although it was interesting to see so many different breeds living together in one place, they were nothing compared to the thumbs I'd just wiggled out from under. She'd tried to explain the reason for the extra precautions, but I'd cut her off gently. Apparently, she wasn't used to people not being curious about the natives.

"I don't want to be rude, but it's not important for me to know that much about Havenwood Falls, because I don't plan on staying long and I probably won't ever come back."

I startled Addie with my candor. Her eyes widened, and her mouth turned down on one side as she mulled over what I'd said. "How do you know you won't be here long?"

The answer was simple. "I can't afford to be here long. I have things to attend to at home. Family issues."

She nodded her head. Family issues. The universally understood term for *don't pry any further into that subject.*

"So, what then? You think you are going to find your mate and then what? Take her with you when you go? What if she has a life here? What if she doesn't want to go?"

"She will definitely want to go. The mate pull is too strong. If I leave, she'll follow. There are no other choices."

Addie chewed on that thought for a moment, quietly looking me in the eyes to assess my character outside of the words I spoke. "Do you think to take her against her will?"

Her entire body was still, and I was reminded that while she posed a very nonthreatening person physically, my answer could very well have me tossed out of this town on my ass.

I was speaking to a very important person.

But it didn't matter. Honesty is one of my most prized virtues, and I had nothing to hide. About my upbringing or my motives.

"Absolutely not." I wouldn't need to. That's not how our mates worked. And even if the situation was different, I would never force someone to be with me. That's Neanderthal behavior, and I had the blood of the gods running through my veins. I wasn't an animal. Mostly.

My beast shifted inside my body at the thought. *You know what I mean.* I sent the words to him silently. Shifter I was. King Asshole I was not.

"How do you know she'll go willingly? That's a hell of a lot of confidence." There was no mistaking the sarcasm in her voice.

"It's not confidence. It's biology. She's my mate. Once we've bonded, that's all she wrote. I don't make the rules, Ms. Beaumont, but I'll enforce them if I need to."

"Opportunist."

Maybe she was right. Maybe I was taking advantage of the situation and making the rules act in my favor. But I wasn't kidding when I said I had family business to attend to, and it trumped anything else on my plate. Except finding my mate. Finding Hannah was actually a key part of the family business I had to attend to, so it all worked out in the end. Whatever we did, it needed to happen quickly. Not just because of my timeline, but because the longer two mates waited to complete the bond, the more it ate away at them. The blood of the gods was a blessing and a curse. Probably. The only information I could find about it with my kind was the book I found that nobody wanted me to read. The one that changed my whole outlook and started this little revolution. Everything that happened to me from the moment I succumbed to the mate pull was a hypothesis.

Probably. The information was a little sketchy at best. And that information, or lack thereof, was a pivotal part of my *family issues.*

She dropped the subject and just bent over my arm, working quietly on the tattoo. Being incredibly meticulous for something that was only going to last for the length of time I was a guest of Havenwood Falls. She stayed that way, silent and diligent, until she stopped to ask me about why I had that creepy smile on my face. She may have acted like she was focused on her work, but she was watching me the entire time, gauging what kind of person I was.

Addie Beaumont was a professional judge of character, and not to be dicked around with.

So I wondered why she hadn't asked the one thing I would think was the most important bit of information to glean from a visitor to Havenwood Falls that required registration. Not once in her questioning or quiet contemplation had she asked me what kind of supe I was. Could she tell? No way. Most people didn't even know shifters like my family existed. I didn't know how progressive Havenwood Falls was, but I was pretty confident in my ability to stay hidden if I wanted to. So, when Addie finished my tattoo, cleaned it and wrapped it, then opened her mouth to ask her next question, I was completely surprised by the words that came out of her mouth.

"How did you know to look for Havenwood Falls?"

I didn't really know how to answer that. "I didn't."

"What do you mean, you didn't? We may be a tourist destination, but no one is here without a purpose. And if you don't have a direct connection to this town, you don't just wander in. How did you know we were here? How did you know about the registration process? You didn't even look surprised when I knocked on your door. You were expecting me. So, Mr. Chevayo Walker, someone had to have fed you the information."

She wasn't the spunky young thing that knocked on my door an hour ago. She was a dead serious young woman asking about a possible security breach, and she also just busted out my whole name. Since my parents died, only the elders and my grandfather called me by my full name. If she meant to appear intimidating, despite her innocuous black-framed glasses and diamond nose stud, then she had my attention.

I sighed, defeated. I wasn't about to get into a pissing match with a twenty-something that stood as tall as my nose. This was her town; I was just passing through. There was no need for me to establish an alpha dominance in this situation. I didn't care enough about the outcome to go through the effort.

"Addie, I didn't come here with any other motive than what I've already told you. I didn't even come to Havenwood Falls like you think I did. I followed the scent of my mate, and she happened to be here. When I found out I had a mate, I just left. No plan, no purpose. I pulled up stakes and hauled ass across several states on a *feeling*. Because that's how it is for *my kind*." I put emphasis on the *my kind*, letting that sink in for a moment before continuing my explanation. "I was surprised to meet the two little old ladies outside of town, though. I thought I was going to be driving up that mountain road forever until I went off a cliff or ran smack into the side of the mountain." I wasn't kidding. The roads were crazy, and GPS was just a joke this far into the Colorado mountains.

Addie's head jerked up at my words. "Two little old ladies?"

Something like laughter laced her voice, but I couldn't be sure, because I couldn't see her mouth to see if she was smiling. She had her hand over her lips like she was contemplating something.

"Yeah, two little old ladies that looked exactly alike. Both wearing pink sweatshirts and cross trainers. They were working in their yard when I drove by, and I stopped to see if they needed help. Those ladies are ancient. They really shouldn't be mowing their own grass. Seriously, don't they have family to do that for them? They were eighty if they were a day."

Addie made a small choking noise, and I eyed her suspiciously. Just because I knew the Heimlich didn't mean I wanted to practice it right then.

"I'm telling the truth. You have to know who they are. The little white house is right off the road before you hit the Welcome to Havenwood Falls sign. You can't miss them."

"She must have had a dream . . ." She was muttering to herself, and she wasn't making any sense.

"Excuse me?" So was I under suspicion, or wasn't I? It was really hard to get a read on Addie Beaumont. One minute she was a slightly hippy young twenty-something with some sweet sleeve tats and an abundance of bangle bracelets, and the next she was pinning me to the wall with her words. Now she was mumbling to herself and laughing softly like a crazy person.

I failed to see what was funny.

"Sorry, Chevy." She looked up at me again, looking relaxed for the first time since our meeting. "I think you got taken in by the Sisters McNee." She laughed again and started packing her gear back in her bag. "Don't worry. It's good luck to meet those two old banshees."

Banshees? I don't know why I was surprised—this was Havenwood Falls after all—but I was still floored that I had mowed the grass for a couple of banshees, then been invited in for tea and the best peach pie I'd ever tasted in my life.

"Well, they are the ones that told me about the town and the rules. Since I'm a straightforward guy, I just came in and waited for you to show up. And here you are. I thought banshees were scary? Those two weren't intimidating at all."

Completing her cleanup, Addie finished zipping her case and

stood, a twinkle in her brown eyes behind the lenses of her glasses. "Scary? No, not in my experience. It's good luck to meet a banshee, although they're pretty scary inside of town. Most people consider them an urban legend at this point. There's a story there, you know, but then again, you said you don't care to know any more than you need to about Havenwood Falls, so I'll keep that tidbit to myself."

I narrowed my eyes at her, and she laughed again. "I feel like I should also tell you that the banshees have Celtic nature magic. Their thumbs are as green as any of the other fae around. I can't imagine they would ever need help to control something as mundane as the length of their grass. And their little house on the side of the road? No one in the history of this town has ever just *happened upon it*. You found the sisters because they wanted to be found. And by you. That's good enough for me. I choose to believe everything you've told me today, Mr. Walker. It seems like your situation is complicated, but I respect your honesty and wish you the best of luck. With Hannah, you'll need it, anyway."

She was really going to leave without asking. She had her bag on her arm and her hand on the doorknob already.

"Are you not going to ask what kind of supe I am?" I couldn't believe she would know it, and I couldn't believe she would complete the registration process without it.

"I don't need to ask you," she answered truthfully. "I knew what you were before I started this tattoo. Did you, or did you not, give me a drop of your blood for analysis? That *just* happened."

She was making fun of me, but I couldn't bring myself to be offended. I'd been honest with her, and she was just returning the favor. It was a testament to the sheltered upbringing of my caste that it didn't occur to me anyone would know about my kind. I cleared my throat and hesitated before asking the question. "Have you ever met another like me?"

"Not exactly like you." She smiled sadly, her eyes holding an infinite wisdom that spoke of her experience and authority. Gone was the smiling, joking young girl who was just here to give me a tattoo. In her place was a woman who'd seen and lived through much more than me. I was so concerned with the problems that faced me personally. Addie was in a position where she probably had to deal personally with other people's problems. "I've met many kinds of shifters though. The mate bond is no joke. I believe you when you say she'll follow you. I just wonder if you'll actually want to leave."

"My people are in trouble. I have a responsibility to myself and to them."

Addie paused with her hand on the doorknob, a look of surprise on her youthful face. "Shifter law is something, isn't it? All species handle things differently, and somehow you have to balance the ways of your people with the human ways to maintain your lifestyle. That's why we love Havenwood Falls. As long as you obey the basic rules here, you can stay within the wards, virtually undetected from the outside world. I'm just saying"—Addie opened the door and paused, throwing the words over her shoulder—"it's not a bad place to be if you're trying to lay low and figure things out."

I had the blood of a god running through my veins. Among shifters, my kind was royalty. Born from more than mere legend, made powerful through worship and fervent prayers. I owed it to my caste to bring them the truth and set them free from the tyranny of genetic manipulation.

"One last warning," Addie said before she shut the door to my room behind her. It was a testament to the shock I'd given her that she'd left out this crucial bit of information. "Don't shift here."

"I wouldn't shift in front of other people. I'm not an idiot." I was mildly offended that she would think otherwise.

"No. I mean at all. I think the *in front of other people* is a given, so it didn't occur to me to tell you. If you reveal yourself in front of humans, the penalty is . . . it's bad. You don't want it. Don't do it, just don't. But in your case . . . you are really special. There will be people, not human, that will try to exploit that. Be safe. Do not shift in Havenwood Falls. I think it would be dangerous for you."

I agreed with her and told her I'd be careful. That was our last exchange of words before she disappeared from my room and my sight, leaving me slightly amused by our exchange. I was only in town for a few days. I could keep my skin for that long. Only a teen in the first throes of change lacked that kind of self-control. But she was wrong about one thing.

If I shifted into my other form, I wouldn't be the one in any danger.

CHAPTER 4

HANNAH

"*P*lease don't tell me you called me out here to discuss the crazy monkey sex you had with a tourist. That kind of thing is textworthy, at the maximum," my friend Alina Anand grouched, pushing her dark hair out of her face with one hand, then moving it back to grasp the piping hot cup in front of her. It may have been almost spring in Havenwood Falls, but almost spring was still winter. And in the mountains, it meant snow-covered peaks and bitter winds, even if the green was forcing its spread through everywhere else in the country. And for people who forgot to wear gloves, like my girl Alina did today, a cup of hot joe was the perfect thing to warm her hands up.

If that sugar-laden confection could still be considered coffee.

"Would you like some coffee with your caramel drizzle and whip?" I took a fortifying sip of my Americano, letting the bitter double shot of espresso slide down my throat with a sigh, the drip of half-and-half I poured in just taking the edge off the scalding hot temp. Forget those sweet fluffy drinks. I liked my coffee to bitch-slap me awake in the morning. Even if I'd been up for hours.

And technically it wasn't morning anymore.

"I happen to like my coffee sweet, like my temperament." Alina took a sip with an evil smile. That was the joke. She looked sweet and acted sweet, but Alina had a naughty streak a mile wide. But fun naughty. Not like the other Alina—Alina Roca, who was a total bitch inside and out. *Sweet like her temperament.* I knew better than to take that at face value. I debated whether I should tell her she had whipped cream on the end of her nose but decided against it when she opened her mouth again. "Anyway, you silly biddy, what was so important I had to get out of my warm bed and rush over here?"

Her dark eyes sparkled over the edge of her cup, and I knew she wasn't really irritated with me but giving me a hard time for fun. It was kind of nice to see, actually. When I first met Alina, she was so timid and reserved. She'd led a sheltered life before coming to Havenwood Falls, and it was nice to see her showing some attitude —even if it was to me.

"Gross. I don't want to know about what you and Uncle Gabe do in bed." Uncle Gabe wasn't really my uncle, but we did have some family history, and I loved calling him by that name— especially since he hated it.

Alina echoed my inner thoughts. "He hates it when you call him that."

"Well, he also doesn't like it when I call him Grandpa Gabe, or Dusty Old Vampire Gabe, so beggars can't be choosers. Uncle Gabe it is." Well, technically he wasn't dusty. Not someone as meticulous about their appearance as Gabe. But he was a very, *very* old vampire.

Alina sighed, the sound of one who was rapidly running out of patience with the same tired argument we'd had a hundred times before.

"Relax, Three Wishes," I told her with a grin. Three Wishes was my pet name for her, because she was a djinn, but not the kind of genie from *Aladdin*. She was something else. A completely different kind of supe. It was my way of acknowledging her roots, without saying it at all. For her kind, being outed put them at terrible risk, even in a place as guarded as Havenwood Falls. Me calling her by her nickname was a reminder we were friends. That I valued her. And another way of me saying please don't be mad at me for poking at

Gabe. Not that I was sorry and I wouldn't do it again, because I wasn't. And I would.

"Okay, back to my original point. You didn't call me down here to talk about some rando you took home last night, right?"

"Don't make it sound like it's something I do all the time," I hissed, looking around to see if anyone was listening. Of course, they weren't. This was Coffee Haven, and people didn't come here to eavesdrop on conversations unless their names were Irene Beckett and Biddie Half-Moon. People came down here for coffee, tea, and some bomb-ass blueberry scones.

I took a bite and mumbled around the sweet crumbly goodness. "Last night was like nothing I've ever dealt with. I think someone spelled me."

Alina let her muffin drop out of her hand from where she'd been poised to bite it. She recovered enough to grab it before it bounced off the table and onto the floor.

"What do you mean—" She lowered her voice to a whisper. "What do you mean, spelled?"

"Like I barely even learned his name before I jumped him and followed him home. I couldn't keep my hands off him. It was like I was somebody else. I made an ass out of myself in the Saloon last night, Lina. Damn, I can still feel his hands on me."

"It's not like you to be so into someone. What's his name? Have I met him?"

A wild bolt of jealousy slashed across my chest, and I snapped at her. "No, you don't know Chevy. Why would you know him? He's mine. You have Gabe."

I immediately wished I could take the words back. That wasn't me. I would never say something like that to anyone, much less my friend.

"Alina, that's weird. I don't know why I said that to you. You see? Something's not right." The worst part was I still kind of wanted to smack her lips off for even showing an interest in him.

Alina's eyes were wide, and she slowly nodded. She took a sip from her cup and swished the liquid around in her mouth thoughtfully. "Maybe you were just horny? I mean, spelling sounds like something that might happen at Silk, but not at the Haven Saloon. And even at Silk, it would be consensual or Melaina would have him out on his ass in a second. Probably minus some pieces."

"Oy. I don't want to know why you know that much about what goes on at Silk. This treads into 'you and Uncle Gabe doing the nasty' category. My virgin ears." I wasn't kidding. I'd never stepped foot inside that nightclub for freaky supes before. Mostly because I had no one to go with. That and the owner—Melaina Savage— scared me a little.

Alina wrinkled her nose and took another drink from the oversized mug in her hands. "Grow up, Hannah," she said without heat. "Look, I don't know why you are so concerned about this. Is it so hard to believe you had an intense attraction to someone and spent the night with him? How much had you had to drink? That could have played a factor too, you know."

"Nothing. I hadn't had a single thing to drink yet, Lena." That was the worst part. "There was nothing hampering my decision-making skills. I saw him. I wanted him. I took him. I followed him out of that bar like he was the pied piper of dick. I don't think he even had a drink either. It was the strangest thing. It was like he was waiting there for me. Waiting for me to notice him, and when I did, everything fell right into place."

"And the problem is?"

"The problem, Lena, is that I had zero control over myself around him. It was like someone had given me a love potion or something. I could see nothing but him, taste nothing but him. If he'd told me to run away with him, I would have. That's how intense the feeling was."

Alina looked thoughtful, like she was studying the various pieces of artwork on the walls, when in reality she was just trying not to make eye contact with me. My best friend wasn't very confrontational, so it surprised the hell out of me when she murmured, "Maybe that's what you need."

"Come again?"

I waited for the common response, *that's what she said*, and then realized that was *my* common response and not Alina's. She wasn't joking. She was serious.

"Okay, Hannah, I will tell you something, and I need you to know it comes from a place of love. But you have an obsessive personality."

"I do not," I sputtered in indignation around a mouthful of crumbs.

"Gross. And yes, you do. Your parents moved out of Havenwood Falls when you were barely an adult. That left you in charge of taking care of Dade with pretty much no familial support. You've taken on the role of a parent to him—which by the way, he's a grown-ass man now so you can let go—and it was your driving force for years until Gabe came back to town."

I tried to cut her off and tell her she was wrong about my adopted brother, but she shushed me with a finger. No one else could get away with that but her, I swear.

"You grew up on your great-granny River's stories, right? When you found out you had the gift of fire like her, she was the one who told you about Jonas and Gabe and how her power was sealed, right? Did she ever sound unhappy about it? Did she ever sound regretful? I'm asking because I wasn't here, Hannah, so I really want to know."

Great-Granny River was a hundred and nine years old when she died. I'm pretty sure she outlived any regrets she might have had, but I couldn't tell Lena that because she just kept talking. Now that she was on a roll, she was talking with her hands, her brown hair flipping around her shoulders and her cup of hot sugar water sloshing dangerously as she flailed.

"From what you've told me, you were fine until Gabriel came back to Havenwood Falls. Suddenly you had someone else to obsess over. In your mind he was the bad guy you needed to focus on, and you've been up his ass ever since. You're lucky we're friends or he would have eaten you by now."

He could try. I'd crisp his ass in a second. I'd never used my power on a person, but I was willing to make an exception for Uncle Gabe. Roasted vampire. Not a bad idea.

"Whatever you're smiling about, knock it off. It's creepy." She knew me too well.

"He has her necklace, Lena. It's a family heirloom."

"She gave it to him, you idiot. He saved her life. Also, in case you missed this part of the story in the one hundred times you heard it growing up, that was *his* necklace. He let Jonas borrow it. For like a half hour. Learn your history."

Satisfied with the dressing down she gave me, Alina took another sip from her cup and grimaced; it was cold now. That's what she got for wasting her time yelling at me instead of drinking her five-dollar coffee essence sugar sludge. I took a drink of my Americano and gagged. Mine was cold too.

"I heard he stole that necklace from a voodoo priestess in New Orleans." I wasn't making that up. I really had heard that.

"Well, that priestess isn't here to corroborate that story, now is she? And we're talking about you, not Gabriel, and your need to bite onto a topic and never let it go. So you are attached on a spiritual level to some excellent dick. I get it. I really do. So maybe just let yourself be that for a little while and see what happens."

I still wasn't happy with—upon closer inspection—her spot-on character assessment of me, and I cringed at her comparing my crazy monkey sex with a religious experience.

"Lena, I don't know . . ."

"Of course you don't. You never know. None of us ever know. Go home. See him again. Have the sex. Give the blow jobs." She couldn't even finish her sentence without blushing and looking around to see if anyone overheard her. Even being a degenerate vampire's lover couldn't erase her sheltered upbringing.

"Oh, I'll go home and blow something all right," I told her with a wicked smile on my face. She smiled back, because she knew exactly what I meant. I was going home to do what I did when I needed to get any good thinking done.

It was time to light stuff on fire and play with it.

CHAPTER 5

CHEVY

*E*ven if Addie hadn't told me where to find Hannah, I would have sniffed her out.

The door to the Hey, Nice Glass shop was painted in bright colors, and the large front windows sported blown glass art pieces in every shape and color.

My girl was an artist and owned her own business. Very cool. And the shop was across the street from Whisper Falls Inn. That was hilarious. She tried so hard to run away from me, and this was as far as she got. Excitement swept through my chest, and my beast reared his head. He wanted to see her too. The more I learned about Hannah, the more I wanted to know. And not in the little bits and pieces I gathered here and there. The need to understand her on the most intimate level pressed down on me from all sides. Obsession. I inhaled it greedily and followed the overwhelming instinct to chase down my mate. The beast inside me agreed—there would be no argument from either of us.

I opened the door, and a little bell jingled overhead. She was here —I smelled her. But she was not the one to greet me when I opened the door. The guy didn't look surprised to see me at all, which was shocking, considering he was wiping down glass ornaments that were hanging from the ceiling by steel cords. There was a ladder set up under the glass, but it wasn't supporting him. Nope. The twenty-something curly-haired young man in the old-school Aquaman T-shirt was floating about six inches above the rungs, defeating the purpose of having a ladder at all.

I mowed a banshee's grass yesterday. This kind of thing did not faze me.

"Should you really be doing that out here in the open like that?"

"I do what I want in my house." He stuck the rag in his back pocket and floated to the floor until he was standing in front of me. "I've got the ladder there if I need a prop. Besides, I saw you through the window. You're the guy who has a boner for my sister."

I'd never seen a guy smile and say the word boner and sister in the same sentence before. I didn't know how to take this kid—he was strange.

"Hannah's your sister?" No sense denying what he said, no matter how awkwardly he put it. Kids these days. Well, he wasn't wrong; if he was Hannah's brother, then I definitely had a boner for his sister. Three already today, in fact.

"I'm Dade. Welcome to Hey, Nice Glass." I took the offered hand, and he pumped it enthusiastically. I could sense no malice from this kid. He was like a happy puppy.

"That's an interesting name. Let me guess, it was Hannah's idea?" I didn't know her that well, but her sass and spunky personality were all over that sign out front. Dade grinned wider, if that was even possible.

"Actually, it was mine. Hannah wanted to call it Blow It Out Your Glass, but the Havenwood Falls Architectural Review Committee quashed it. Said it wasn't indicative of the family-friendly environment of the Town Square Business District, so she couldn't have a sign hanging out front."

I thought Blow It Out Your Glass was an awesome name.

"You said you recognized me. Have we met?" I know he saw me approaching the store through the big glass window, but how did he know I had a connection to Hannah? I'd just met her last night, and I didn't remember seeing him since I'd come to Havenwood Falls. He didn't look like a Court spy. Not that I would recognize one anyway.

"I was at the Haven Saloon last night. Hannah and I go together after work all the time. She also whoops Benny's ass every time too. He thinks if he challenges her enough, someday he'll be able to take the punch."

Benny must have been the giant guy she sent flying. He hadn't seemed too bent about it. That must have been why.

"Is he a supe too?" He would have to be to keep taking hits like that every day.

"Nope. Totally human. Just a big dumb one." Dade pulled the rag back out of his pocket and looked up at all the decorative glass bulbs hanging from the ceiling. I bet that was a bitch to clean on the regular. "I saw the moment you walked in the bar. We'd only been there a few minutes. Then you came in, and it was like a radio signal to her brain. She popped old Benny for a loop and left me at the table. It was kind of funny to watch."

This kid had a warped sense of humor if he thought the weird shit that went on with the mate bond was any kind of funny.

"And you weren't concerned about your sister at all? I just took her out of the bar without a word to any of you."

The kid smiled again and floated back up to continue the work he'd been doing when I first walked in.

"From what I saw, it looked like she took you for a walk, man. My sister is grown and can handle herself. Also, she's going to be pissed I let you in, but since I live to mess with her, you can find her if you go back through that door over there." He jerked his thumb over his shoulder, and I saw said door. "I would be careful not to be too noisy, though. She's working."

I was intrigued. I would love to see Hannah working. Or doing nothing at all even. I just wanted to see Hannah.

"Why would you send me back there if you know she doesn't want to see me? Aren't you afraid of making her mad?"

"You've met Hannah. She's always mad. Besides, riling up my older sister is my prerogative as a bratty younger brother."

"You realize you're a grown-ass man, right?" He was younger than me, but still.

His laughter followed me through the heavy dark doorway but cut off when I closed the door behind me.

Dade was right about both things. Hannah was working, and she was not happy to see me.

She must have heard me coming, because her back was to me as she bent over her workstation, tiny streams of fire spurting out from some unseen source and curling around the glass she held in her hands, sans gloves.

"No one is supposed to be back here." The words floated over her shoulder as if she couldn't be bothered to turn around and look at me. I'd been fine with just waiting for her, but seeing her in the semi-lit room wearing nothing but a tank top and cut-off booty shorts, most likely because of the heat in the studio, bled my self-control. Desire surged through the mate bond and Hannah shimmered in front of my eyes, a sensual mirage.

Beautiful mate.

"I'm not no one," I countered, my words thickened with desire. It happened so fast. Just seeing Hannah had my libido going zero to sixty. My dick was going to break off if I didn't quit giving it a workout.

She still hadn't turned to look at me.

"What do you want from me?"

I shifted my trajectory and instead of walking up behind her, I came up to her from the side, and for the first time, I got a clear view of what she was working on. It was a little glass bird with rainbow-colored wings.

The irony of the project was not lost on me. If she only knew how fucking close she was right now to everything. I'd seen glasswork before. I'd seen fused glass and blown glass, and it looked like this studio was set up for blowing. There was a kiln in the corner and curious equipment strewn around. Hannah did not keep a tidy shop, but some people were like that. Sometimes the most beautiful art was created from chaos. I envied those who could bring it out. I was too analytical for art. I was a numbers guy, but I still liked to look at pretty things. I was looking at something beautiful right now, in fact.

"I want to watch you work." It wasn't a lie. I wanted a lot of things, but that could technically be classified as one of them. I didn't *not* want to watch her work, so that counted.

"Suit yourself."

And then she did it. That thing I'd never seen another person do outside of a circus tent, and even then I knew the science of it. This was not science nor an illusion. This was something different.

She didn't blow glass, air through a tube, or anything. She blew fire.

From her mouth.

Completely ignoring me as I watched, she inhaled, filling her lungs, and blew like she was snuffing out a candle. But the line of fire shot out of her mouth in a molten thread and curled around the piece she was working on, softening the glass in just the right places as she poked and prodded with her tools, bending the piece until it fit her vision.

I'd never seen anything so cool in my entire life, and I could change into an animal. Hannah blowing fire turned my simmering desire into a raging inferno.

"I can smell you, you know. I can tell how you're feeling." She sounded irritated.

If she turned to look at me, she could see how I was feeling too. My erection tapped the back of my zipper so hard, I thought it was going to rip a hole in my pants. *Sexy mate.*

"How are you doing that?" she whispered, still focusing on her project.

"Doing what?" Getting hard?

"How are you making me feel like this? I don't even know you."

Oh. *Oh, that.* The mate bond. Her body had to be going nuts being this close. I know mine was. She sure didn't show it, though—just stood there bent over her work, arms shaking.

Oh, there it was. That was some marvelous self-control. From what I understood, although I was no expert, as soon as mates recognized each other, the attraction became so intense, the two had no choice but to couple—and often. The only way to relieve the stress of the bond was to solidify it, through lots and lots of steamy sex.

From what I understood.

"What do you know about shifters and mates, Hannah?" My voice was soft, and she flinched when I said her name.

"I know several shifters. I know I'm not one, and I'm also not a mate."

"False. You are a mate. You're mine."

"That's bullshit. I don't even know you." She finally turned to look at me, and I wanted to look her right in her angry eyes, but I couldn't. I swear I tried, but Hannah was not wearing a bra under that flimsy spaghetti-strap tank top, and her breasts were right there, in my face. I could see her nipples through the thin cloth of the shirt for fuck's sake, and as she caught my line of sight they hardened, the little nubs poking through, just begging me to pay attention.

"God damnit," she muttered. Biology. It didn't lie.

She whirled around again, putting her back between me and her work, but it was too late. I saw how she responded to me, and I was going to take advantage of it.

She stiffened as I shifted. Instead of standing next to her, I placed my body directly behind her, so I could feel her heat through her clothes.

"You don't have to turn around, just listen." I spoke gently, soothing. I was also close enough to breathe into her ear, and she shuddered. Yeah, I knew what I was doing, but she hadn't pushed me away yet, so I pressed on. "I get it. It's scary. You've never felt like this before, and it's terrifying. Your body reacts a certain way to me, and you feel like you have no control over it."

I reached one hand around and slid my palm over the gentle swell of one breast. Her breath caught in her throat.

"If you don't like it, Hannah, tell me no. Push me away. But I don't think you can. Otherwise, keep working. I'll tell you what I can."

She said nothing, but let out her breath in a little whoosh and picked up her tools again. I took that as a sign to continue.

"I hate you," she whispered. But she shifted her weight and leaned into my hand, giving me permission to explore further. My other hand slid up her thigh, toward the ragged hem of her way-too-short-for-public shorts. So short the pockets hung out and my fingers barely had any distance to go at all before they were sliding over the already damp cotton of her panties. She was already wet for me. No matter how angry, her body wanted this as badly as mine did.

"Hate is such a strong word, Hannah." I pinched one nipple through the thin layer of her tank, and she responded by spreading her legs ever so slightly, giving me better access to the place between them.

She moaned even as she tried to focus on her task, that thin stream of flame blowing from between her lips again, directing the heat against the glass wings of the bird on the table.

"Your body is amazing, Hannah. And I know how scary it is for you, because it's the same for me. My people? You don't know them. You don't know any of us, but we don't have mates like other shifters do. Or we didn't think we could. We've been lied to our whole lives. None of us have ever felt the mate bond before—Hannah, if you wiggle like that, I'll lose my train of thought."

She was pressing back now, her ass pushing against my swollen cock, held back by the confining layer of my pants. She didn't answer, just pretended to focus on her task. Her mind may have been distracted, but her body was definitely with me on this thing.

"You know how they did it? The elders of my kind? Drugs, Hannah. They suppressed the mate bond with drugs. All in the name of pure breeding. What if a mate was a wolf shifter? Or a fae?

For our kind, purity of the bloodline is the highest priority. Continuation of the species. Matches are carefully decided, based on genetics and family history. Mates got in the way, so they made it so we never sensed them. Never found each other." I rained kisses down her shoulder, letting my tongue taste the beads of sweat on her skin, and my fingers slid under the barrier of her panties and into the wet heat of her sex.

She bit back a scream.

The conversation was serious, but our bodies were discussing something altogether different. Project abandoned, Hannah let the fire die from her lips and closed her eyes. One hand braced her weight against the table in front of us and the other slid over the front of her shorts to cup the place where my busy fingers searched.

Yes, Hannah. Show me how to touch you.

"Why couldn't I feel you before now?" The words seemed hard to get out, and they should have been. Her breath was coming faster and faster as I palmed her breast again, working it with my hand until she bucked against me. The tremors were already starting in her legs.

"I think it has something to do with the wards around Havenwood Falls." My own breath was hard to come by, and only a massive amount of self-control kept me from ripping her shorts off and burying my dick inside her. I wanted to possess her. I wanted to own her. My beast agreed. "But what about now, Hannah? I'm here now. Can you feel me?"

I didn't expect an answer, and I didn't get one. Not verbally anyway. But her hand pressed harder against mine as my fingers pistoned into her body and my thumb made small flicking motions against her clit with every pass.

It was a dick move, but I wasn't above using predatory means. Neither of us could fight this, and it was only going to get worse the longer she struggled.

"Hannah, I asked you a question. Can you feel me now?" I pulled her hard against me, the hand that was fondling her breast moving to her neck. Not squeezing, but possessing, just how she liked it. I got that peek into her preferences last night. Hannah was a difficult girl to deal with. Her mind wanted to be the boss, but her body wanted to be owned.

I was the right man for the job.

She sobbed her release behind closed lips and clenched teeth. Barely a sound escaped her mouth even as I felt the vibrations through the fingers I had wrapped around her throat. I held her there for a few seconds, not exerting any pressure—just holding her. The humiliation would set in soon. The anger. I would deal with it then. But right now, I let her lean against me as she came down from that amazing high, the mating bond appeased for the moment. For her, anyway.

I needed more.

"Hannah, I want you to talk."

She tried to twist around to look at me but my hand on her neck refused to let her turn. "What?"

"I want to hear your voice. Did that feel good? Don't lie to me. I'll know." I tugged at the waistband of her denim shorts. They were so loose around her waist, I didn't even need to unfasten them. They pulled right down and pooled at her feet. Hannah moaned low and shifted her stance, but kept her head bent low and didn't say a word. "Hannah, do you want me to stop?"

I'd asked her that before, and I felt the same way as I did then. I'd give her the right to stop me, but I'd die if she did. And just like before, she let the opportunity pass her by.

"I didn't hear you, Hannah. Do you want me to stop?" Emboldened by her lack of refusal, I unsnapped my jeans and pulled them down, my erection springing free and bouncing off her lower back. She shuddered in response. "Hannah."

"Don't stop." So quiet. That really wouldn't do.

"Hm?" I wasn't being an asshole on purpose. I just needed, on a cellular level, to hear her say the words.

"Don't stop touching me." There was my approval, and her voice was husky with need. My dick jerked in response.

"How do you want me to touch you?"

"Do we really have to do this?" Her fury was evident in every syllable.

"Yes. We do. Because your posture indicates I'm forcing you, but that's not the case at all. I get that you're angry, and I understand you're confused, but you can't hide your body's response. So if you want any part of me to touch any part of you"—I ran my tongue from the crack of her ass up to the back of her neck in one solid line, then pulled away abruptly—"you'll tell me, in explicit detail, exactly what you want me to do. All you have to do is say the words, Hannah. We've been through this. I'm yours to command. Tell me."

"What if I can't say it?" she whispered while twisting under my grasp. She could have escaped my hold. I was barely holding her down. I was on to her now. She loved being restrained.

"You can say anything to me, Hannah. I won't judge you. I want to give you what you need."

"Just do it."

"Do what?" She wasn't going to get away with that half-assed response.

"You know."

"No, I don't, Hannah. Do what?"

She growled in frustration and bucked against the table, pushing back until her ass was grinding on my exposed cock, and I had to brace myself to keep from taking us both down to the floor.

"Fuck me, okay? I want you to fill me up. It's all I've been thinking about since I left your room this morning, and it pissed me off. I don't want to need anyone, but my body can't calm down if you're not around. So if it will give me five fucking minutes of peace, then fuck me, but I don't want anything slow and romantic. Give it to me hard. As hard as you can, because I'm feeling aggressive."

I almost lost my load right there, and I wasn't even inside her yet. She had no idea the effect her words had on me. As much as she liked me whispering in her ear last night, she couldn't have any clue what her violent request did to me.

So I showed her.

The hand holding the back of her neck moved down to her

waist, and I mirrored my grip on the other side, steadying her for a moment before I entered her hard from behind. If she hadn't been ready, it might have hurt, but after the stroking and teasing from before, she was primed and ready to receive me. I would have liked to have lasted longer, but I couldn't hold back anymore, slamming into her repeatedly as she bent lower over the work table, lifting her ass higher so I could hit her in all the right places.

"Yes," she moaned as she rested her face in her folded arms. "I need this. I need you."

I bet she didn't even know what she was saying, but I understood. We both needed it. The mate bond demanded our sacrifice, and would torture us endlessly until we provided satisfaction. That aching, itchy need would continue until we appeased nature. I finished in silence, my own release as violent as hers, bearing down to the music of my skin slapping the back of her thighs and the creaking of the table underneath as I slammed into Hannah one last time. She straightened when I pulled away, grabbing some shop towels from a roll on a nearby table to clean herself. After a moment she handed the roll to me as well.

All business. She wouldn't even look me in the eyes.

The intense need from moments ago dwindled away to guilt, and I took the towels from her silently, cleaning myself and throwing them in the trash. We dressed in silence as well. No one knew what to say after such a violent clash of bodies and will. I was just trying to explain things to her, and it spiraled out of control. Now I just felt dirty. I never wanted anything I did with Hannah to feel dirty. I opened my mouth to say something, anything, but no words were forthcoming.

"Can you just leave now?" My heart twisted at the raw vulnerability in Hannah's voice.

"Hannah, I know you think I'm doing this to you on purpose, but I'm not. I don't have any experience with this either. I just know that we can't fight it. If we try, the results will be dire. I don't know just how bad it will get, but I also don't want to push the envelope.

You're my mate, Hannah, and until you accept that, it's only going to get worse. For both of us."

I didn't say anything else. She didn't want me to. She wasn't going to look at me again, and I didn't have anything else to say that would make her feel better.

So I left, but I would be back. She just needed some time. I shut the door to the sound of her crying, feeling like the biggest dick.

This mate shit was hard. There wasn't anything in the book about a situation like this.

CHAPTER 6

HANNAH

*T*he Haven Saloon was pretty dead even for a weekday night, but it was the end of April after all, and there weren't many tourists that wanted to deal with the crazy range in temperature, or the snow turned slush turned just plain wet. I mean, we never really had a "dead" time, but there were busy seasons and busier seasons, and this just wasn't it.

That's the only reason I eyeballed the door with apprehension every time someone walked through it. Just because I took notice— not because I was expecting anyone.

Lies.

I was expecting two someones, and lucky me, the first one was right on time.

Adrian Roca. My best frenemy.

I wouldn't call us close, and I wouldn't call us friends, but we did have a connection. A business connection. Well, to be clear, Adrian wanted to have a business connection. He owned the Circle J pot dispensary in Havenwood Falls, and he had been hounding me for a long time to supply him with some custom glass pipes for his shelves. I don't have anything against smoking. I really don't.

It's just that blowing glass pipes is so *boring*. Seriously. It isn't fun. Some people like it, but I was much more into free form glass, and designing big-eyed aliens or a glass animal with a mouthpiece on its butt just didn't do it for me. So I always told him no.

Until now.

I had something he wanted, and now there was something I wanted from him. *Please, please let this work.* I was desperate.

His gray-green eyes met mine across the dim bar, and he strode toward my table with a purpose, his mouth set in a firm line. He didn't like it. He didn't want to do it.

But he was going to all the same.

I hadn't seen Chevy since he left me standing in the shop yesterday afternoon, a quivering mess barely able to stand on my own. The humiliation still burned in my chest. He hadn't tried to contact me in a whole night and day, but he would. He'd promised he would. So I called Adrian for help.

Tall, dark, and handsome he was; he might have been my type if he wasn't almost ten years my junior. And a local. Two strikes against him, and the third was that smart mouth of his. There was only room for one sarcastic wit in a relationship, and it belonged to me. So no, I would never consider Adrian Roca dating material—but we sure as hell would be pretending tonight.

Because Chevy Walker wasn't taking no for an answer, and I didn't know if I was strong enough to keep saying it by myself.

That's where Adrian came in.

"I don't know why you're asking me to pretend to be your next conquest, Hannah, and to be honest, it feels like bullshit to me, but I'm holding you to your end of the bargain regardless." His mouth pulled down at the corners as he spoke, and he tossed his navy jacket over the back of the corner booth and sat down next to me heavily.

I got it. I didn't like it either. Actually, a small wave of revulsion rippled through me as he sat next to me and his denim-clad thigh brushed my own. My stomach twisted into a tight knot and then released almost before I could even register the pain.

God, I hoped I wasn't coming down with something.

"What kind of cologne are you wearing?" I wasn't trying to gag on the stench, honestly, but whatever he had sprayed himself with, it was doing Adrian Roca no favors. He was a handsome enough guy —all of the Rocas were—but if he kept wearing whatever he doused himself with tonight, he'd find himself all alone. I don't know why I was even worried about it. Tonight he was supposed to be with me. In theory anyway. My guts recoiled at the thought.

Jesus, Hannah, what's wrong with you?

Adrian lifted his arm and sniffed conspicuously. "Soap?" A puzzled expression covered his face. "I took a shower and used regular soap. I don't wear cologne. That's kid shit."

I couldn't help but laugh at him. "You are twenty-three years and like, five minutes old. You don't get to use the *kids* excuse."

I punched him softly in the arm to take the sting out of my words. He grimaced and rubbed the spot.

Shit. It's not that Adrian Roca was weak. Far from it. The moroi vampires had no problem with strength, as far as I knew. But I was a descendant of rock trolls on my great-grandfather's side. I didn't shift like Papa Jonas, but I sure as shit had some of his strength. I kind of forgot sometimes.

Adrian continued talking like I hadn't just left a baseball-sized bruise on his bicep, not because he was too manly to admit that I'd just punched right through his masculinity, but because deep down under his sarcastic bad-boy demeanor, he wasn't a complete asshole and he knew I was sensitive about my strength.

"You might be ten years older than me, *Hannah Banana*," he said, using the nickname I'd hated since I was little, "but you still look like you're twelve, and you did just ask *this kid* for a favor." Then he surprised me by leaning in close, almost too close for my comfort, and swooping in for a perfectly chaste peck on the cheek. "Now give Daddy some sugar."

Ugh. Gross. Why couldn't I even pretend to like Adrian Roca? There was nothing, and I mean *nothing*, wrong with him.

But my gorge still rose when his lips touched my cheek.

The thunder cracked so loudly outside, even Bent Brent looked up from behind the bar, startled. It had been dry as a bone all day with no rain in the prediction, but it wasn't the rain on the wind I scented.

It was sweet. It was mellow. It was smooth like caramel or honey.

I'd lay a fiver Chevy Walker was standing outside the front door of the Haven Saloon.

If I'd actually made that bet, I would be five dollars in the hole, because as soon as Adrian moved away from me, a small frown between his eyebrows, I saw the figure looming directly behind him. Eyes dark and flashing, the cords of his neck straining with his obvious distemper.

Chevy was angry.

Angry Chevy was divine.

Absolutely not, I chastised myself vehemently. *I don't want to be attracted to him. I don't want to be bound to him. I don't want him to be right.* I took small, shallow breaths even though every part of me was screaming to fill my lungs with the warm scent of him. My entire body tightened with the effort.

Adrian noticed. "Is this the guy that's been bothering you, babe?"

I had to give him credit—Adrian covered my agitation like a smooth operator even if I did bristle at the word *babe* coming out of his mouth. I had to remind myself that I *wanted* him to act this way toward me. I had to make Chevy see he had no power over me. That I had moved on. I couldn't be infatuated with him if I was sleeping with someone else, right?

Adrian put his arm around my shoulder, and I tried like hell not to shrink away from him as he squeezed me close. *He must really want those pipes for his store.* Hell, if he held me any tighter, I would be in his lap. I snuck a look up at Chevy from under my lashes; he caught me. The frown on his face grew even more menacing, and I tried not to let my eyes wander past the expanse of his shoulders in that dove gray thermal shirt he wore. His tan skin showed dark against the soft, washed-out color of his shirt. He had the sleeves shoved up his forearms.

It was like kryptonite for my eyes.

He saw me looking, and the grim line of his mouth changed to a wide smile. His teeth were perfect and white. Of course they were. I immediately broke eye contact and looked away, snuggling under Adrian's arm and trying not to heave as waves of nausea rolled through my body.

I was asking him to do this. This was what I wanted.

But my body rebelled.

"What are you doing, Hannah?" The smile was gone, but the frown hadn't returned. Chevy just stood there, jacket slung over his arm like a waiter with a white towel. He stood there patiently, like he was waiting to be asked to sit with us. But we wouldn't do that. I wanted him to go away, didn't I?

I want him to take me away.

Where the hell had that thought come from? I hated my traitor body and its apparent need to drape itself over Chevy every time he showed up. Mates my ass. Destiny my ass. Bow to his beck and call? *My ass.*

"I'm doing whatever I want to, Chevy. Two days ago, it happened to be you. Today, I've moved on to a newer model." I felt more than heard Adrian snort beside me, his chest vibrating against my shoulder with his obvious effort to keep from laughing. Yeah, I know it was a bad line. Acting wasn't my strong suit. But even if it was lame, he should have taken the hint.

Who wouldn't take the hint?

Apparently, Chevy Walker was thick as a box of bricks because instead of getting angry and leaving . . .

He sat down.

At the table. Next to me. On the other side of me in the corner booth, effectively creating a Hannah sandwich. But the bread on one side was a man I was trying like hell not to be drawn to, and the other one I was trying like hell to pretend I liked.

I struggled to keep away from Chevy when all I wanted to do was crawl into his lap and stay there. Instead I plastered myself to Adrian's body as hard as I could. Harder still, until I felt him squirming beside me. It was probably taking all of his balance to keep his butt cheeks plastered to the booth seat with me shoving against him with all my might. What a sight we must have looked, but this was a game of mental tug of war and I would be damned if Chevy Walker would pull me back over to his side without a fight.

I mean *at all*.

His frown changed to another smile, but it was not a nice smile. This smile was all white teeth and thinned lips. This smile was crafty and cunning and not at all like what I had seen on his face before. In all our two days of knowing each other. I didn't like it. I almost reached out to smooth it off his face but caught myself with my hand in midair.

Chevy smiled wider.

"What's your name, kid?" Oh shit, he just called Adrian *kid*.

"It's Adrian, and I'm not taking the bait even though I would love to knock your teeth in. Hannah doesn't want to be around you, and as you can see, she's with me now, so why don't you take the hint and fuck off?" Adrian said he wasn't taking the bait, but the look on his face said he was already fantasizing about the fight that was coming. *Such a Roca.* They were always game for a fight.

"That's a pretty juvenile attitude, even for someone as young as you, don't you think, Adrian?" Chevy was mocking us, I could tell, and the red heat of rage flooded my body. So hot, in fact, that my skin began to tingle and my vision swam a bit. I wasn't calling my fire right now, so why was I so flushed? Feverish even?

It was all Chevy's fault. Probably. I pushed even harder under Adrian's arm, much like a cat head-butting his owner's hand. Adrian paused for a moment but then squeezed me with affection.

I wanted to throw up.

"Hannah, you feel hot. Are you okay? Do you need to step outside?" Adrian sounded worried, but I wasn't worried. I would be fine as long as Chevy promised to leave me alone.

"If I step foot outside of this bar, he's gonna have me right where he wants me." My words sounded slurred even to me, but that couldn't be right. "Don't let him get me, kid." Whoops. I called Adrian kid too. Maybe he didn't notice.

"What the hell's wrong with you, Hannah? Something isn't right."

Adrian needed to mind his beeswax. I would be just fine if he would start manning up to his side of the agreement. And I wish he would move his arm. Why did it feel so gross when he touched me? My thoughts were chaotic, contradicting. I needed air.

"Hannah, don't do this. This is the hard way. We both know how this has to end up. Please don't fight. I don't want to see you hurting."

Stupid Chevy and his stupid sexy voice. I wished he would shut up and keep talking to me. Or something. Damnit.

"Shut up, you handsome asshole. I'm having sex with . . ."—I fumbled for the name—"this guy now."

Adrian groaned next to me. I heard him whispering under his breath, "Jesus, Hannah. This is a shitshow."

"Okay then, show me." I'm pretty sure that's what Chevy said, but there was no way I heard him correctly.

"Say what now?"

I echoed Adrian's sentiment. "Yeah, say what now?"

The room was spinning, and the heat suffusing my skin was damn near unbearable, which was weird, considering I was technically fireproof. But one thing remained stable in the fisheye lens of my vision, and that was Chevy's very white, very wide, and very scary smile.

"You're being difficult on purpose, Hannah. I don't know who Adrian is to you, but you're putting him in a really awkward position. He's worried. Pretty soon other people in this bar are going to be worried. But I'll humor you for about twenty more seconds before I take over this show. How far are you willing to take this charade, Hannah?" Chevy slapped his hand on the table hard enough to make me jump. Adrian didn't jump, though. He just sighed with what sounded like relief. I don't know what he had to be relieved about. This wasn't going according to plan at all. "If you're intent on proving it's real, then why don't you go ahead and kiss him, *mate*? Go on. Kiss him right on the lips. Right in front of me."

Chevy lowered his voice then, so only Adrian and I could hear him even though every eye in the bar was on our little corner. "But don't be surprised if I kill him afterward."

Adrian didn't miss a beat. "Did he say *mate*?" Adrian hissed a few curses under his breath. "That's shifter shit, Hannah. You didn't say anything about mates."

Chevy smiled again. "Of course she didn't."

Adrian's arm immediately left my side, and he jumped out of the booth so fast I almost fell out as well, but Chevy's hand on my arm kept me from completely losing my balance.

God, his touch felt so calming. So good.

I immediately shook him off.

"Adrian, get back here and be my boyfriend," I whisper-yelled, trying not to cause a scene and failing miserably. I heard some laughter from somewhere in the bar, but my vision was too swirly to see where it came from.

"Look, Hannah, you're a mess. I'm canceling the agreement. I don't need your glass. I mean, I want it," he amended, "but I'm not doing whatever . . . this is. I'm not getting into an alpha battle of who has the most chest hair with someone who obviously knows what's going on better than you do. Also, if I touch you again, I think you might really throw up this time. I'm not fucking or feeding you, and you lied to me about what's going on here. I don't owe you shit. Handle your business."

I grasped the air angrily, but Adrian quickly moved out of my way.

"Smart kid." Chevy smiled that *not happy at all* smile again. I didn't like it.

"Look. We get it. You're her mate. You can stop whatever is happening right now, but obviously she's fucking terrified or she wouldn't be acting like this. So maybe you could not be a dick and take care of Hannah instead of pissing in a circle around her. But if you really want to fight . . ." Adrian rolled his shoulders and smiled. The same kind of not *happy at all* smile Chevy had been sporting since they started their standoff. "I could use the exercise."

"Fair enough."

Oh no, they were not having some sort of macho man agreement right in front of me.

"I'm not going with you, Chevy Walker."

"Oh yes, you are, Hannah Pederson." And then he kissed me. Hard. On the mouth.

And my traitor body loved it. Loved it so much I opened my mouth by accident and his tongue swept inside, ripping a moan from my throat. Before I could catch myself, my arms wrapped around his neck, and I pushed my tongue against his, dancing, licking, biting on his lip. It was seconds, no, hours later when we pulled apart, and there was that damn smile again.

"Hannah, I win."

"The hell you say."

The world tipped upside down, and before I could blink, Chevy had scooped me up with both arms. If I thought he was going to carry me like a princess, I was sadly mistaken. The gentle hold lasted about four seconds before I was slung unceremoniously over his shoulder, my face against the small of his back, right above the tight swell of his butt that looked completely bitable through his dark wash jeans.

Damnit. He got me.

"Should we help her?" someone asked from across the bar.

"No, she's good." Adrian was doing a shit job of protecting me. I should have asked someone else.

"Say goodnight, Hannah." Chevy was infuriatingly cheerful. I couldn't see his face, but I would have bet he was sporting a real smile now. He sounded really happy.

"Goodnight Hannah," I mocked him aggressively, and he laughed. The whole rest of the bar laughed, actually. They were all against me. Bunch of drunk assholes. Even though I was angry, I had to admit now that Adrian was no longer touching me, I felt better. Actually, now that Chevy held me, I felt almost normal, even with his sticky sweet smell filling my lungs, making me think dirty things as he walked toward the bar entrance, his shoulders flexing under my thighs. I clenched them together to keep them from trembling.

He responded by gripping my legs tighter. And whistling.

I turned my head to the side, and the last thing I saw before the doors closed on us both was Bent Brent behind the bar waving, a dazed smile on his face. I lifted a hand and waved back weakly.

There was no one to save me now. The devil had me in his hands.

CHAPTER 7

CHEVY

*D*on't cause trouble. Do no harm to anyone in Havenwood Falls. Don't shift in front of humans.

Three rules, and I was in danger of breaking every damn one of them because of a single tiny female. The female that was slung over my shoulder, because it was the most humiliating position I could think to put her in, and she needed some punishment for how she'd just acted.

Unfortunately, it also put her ass right next to my face, and as I walked, her denim-clad rear end grazed my cheek with every step. Up until now I'd exercised damn near iron control, but if you put a feast in front of a starving man, he's going to eat.

And I was ravenous.

Hannah stopped struggling as soon as we left the bar, and as I rounded the corner, contemplating whether to carry her like a caveman back to my hotel room or drag her down a dark alley and have my way with her, she spoke up.

"Where are we going?"

I didn't answer her. I couldn't. The beast inside of me was pressing against my flesh from the inside, and I knew that if push came to shove, it didn't matter what the rules of Havenwood Falls were. My shift was coming and there wasn't much I could do to stop it.

"Chevy, what's wrong? You smell different. I don't know why I know that, but you do. Put me down."

And I did, because I didn't have a choice. I couldn't carry her another step because my insides were screaming for either sex or a shift, and my body wouldn't take me another step unless I made a decision. As soon as her feet touched the ground, Hannah whirled on me, a snarky retort on her tongue, no doubt, but the anger died in her throat as she got a look at my face.

"Chevy, your eyes. They're silver. Why are they silver? Are you going to shift here? You can't shift here. Oh, shit, you can't shift here!" Her eyes darted back and forth in a panic, and she turned in a circle in the middle of the sidewalk, on the corner between Whisper Falls Inn and the glass shop. Then she reached in her pocket, pulled out a set of keys, and clicked the fob once, twice. A bright yellow Jeep street-parked in front of Hey, Nice Glass blinked its headlights in greeting. "Get in the car. Man, I hope it has gas."

I didn't ask any questions. I couldn't form any words. All of my efforts were focused on staying inside my own skin. I begged my beast to reconsider, but he'd been pushed too far. The mate bond was strangling us both, and it either needed the closeness of my mate skin to skin, or I needed to shift and heal a bit before the madness took me over.

Mate sickness. If affected all shifters differently. Lucky for me, I could shift, but if it happened to Hannah . . . I didn't know how horrible it would be. I didn't have anything but that old journal I'd found in the restricted section of the elders' library, but nothing had prepared me for the absolute havoc that was going on inside my body.

"Seriously, Chevy, get in the car." Hannah was running now, dragging me behind her by the arm, and as we got to the Jeep in question, she flung the door open and pushed me inside, her hand hot as a brand on my back. I resisted the urge to push back, just to have the feeling of her touching me again, and struggled to shut the door as she ran around the other side and climbed into the driver's seat.

My body seized, and my breath caught in my throat as Hannah slammed the Jeep into gear and careened out of the parking spot, tires wailing as she took off down the road, around the corner and straight down Main Street. Away from the town square, away from any houses or businesses, straight down the road that would take us out of town. I had no idea where we were going, but I couldn't get out the words to ask, because my throat was closing up and I was almost to the point of being unable to use human speech.

Don't you dare shift in the car. I would destroy the Jeep, and it would be painful for everyone involved.

"You have to shift, right? Hold yourself together just until I get out of town, okay? You need some space, right? How much space do you need? I don't even know what you are. How big do you get? Shit. I just need to get out of town. No people no people no people." In the end she was just chanting, so I closed my eyes and let her ramble. If she was focused on this, at least she wasn't thinking about ways to ditch me, or ways to be defiant. If she was focused on taking care of me, then she was with me, and my beast was slightly mollified by that. Not enough to ease the urge to break free, but at least he wasn't screaming to break free in a moving vehicle.

Hannah's current obedience was buying us a few precious minutes at least. As Main Street curved out of town and began its trek down the mountainside, the buildings disappeared and thick green forest surrounded us on two sides. The trees drowned out the moon, and the only light came from the headlights of the Jeep. I could tell even with my eyes closed, because I was so close to a shift. The eyes of my beast could see through the thickest darkness, even that of my closed eyelids.

Maybe I didn't have as many minutes as I thought.

"Hannah." I ground the word out with maximum effort. My voice was thick, rough and foreign. "Stop the car."

She obeyed immediately, pulling the Jeep over into the soft grass on the side of the road, and thank goodness for small miracles, because something was about to happen and if she was defiant again, I wouldn't be able to control what happened after that. The mate bond was so tense, it stretched between us like a rubber band close to breaking—except this bond wouldn't break. Couldn't break. It could only stress to extreme pain until we both succumbed to the pressure. Hannah wasn't the only one who needed to obey the pull. My body was past what it could endure.

"Hannah. Run."

"What?" she asked, confusion stamped on her face. I couldn't blame her. Nothing that was happening made any sense, but I was too far gone to be able to explain it to her.

It was painful to form the words, but I had to. Had to protect her from what was happening. "Sex or shift, Hannah. I need sex or shift, and I'm past being able to pick which one. I can't control it right now. Please. Run. Now." And then my beast screamed, a bird of prey, and the noise galvanized Hannah into action.

But the minute she slammed the door shut behind her, I was motivated to move as well. My beast wanted sex or shift, but the minute I told her to leave, my body decided what it needed the most. My prey was running, and it was my first and strongest instinct to hunt her down.

Keep going, Hannah. Don't stop, I begged silently even while I tore through the grass and trees, pursuing her relentlessly. She may have been a supe, and she may have been strong, but she was no match for me in speed, even inside my human skin. I smelled her on every blade of grass she stomped on, and the wind told me every change in direction. I could see every move she made like a beacon of light, exposing her trail. A bright shimmering path to follow.

She would not outrun me.

I found her, crouched and gasping next to a tree. She was breathless and sweating, her hair shining brilliant in the darkness, a lit match, a beacon. I didn't stop when I found her, just kept going until I bowled right into her, at least having the presence of mind to roll backwards so when we hit the ground, I went first. I landed on the hard dirt and rolled again, until she was beneath me, her back pressed against the ground and her legs trapped under mine.

"Why didn't you keep going?" She could have. I would have still caught her, but she definitely stopped on purpose. I felt a little better with her body pressed to mine, a little clearer-headed. But her knee bumped against my swollen erection, and I growled involuntarily, pressing my body into hers so there was no mistaking which direction this was going. Shift or sex.

Sex it was.

I didn't want to hurt her, but I had zero control.

"Hannah." One word. It was all I could do.

She freed her arms from underneath me, and I braced myself for the struggle. My beast braced himself for the fight as well, but it didn't come. Instead, those slim arms wrapped around me, and her voice, no longer harsh and angry, whispered in my ear.

"It's all right. Come here. Whatever you need."

What? That wasn't right. She should have been fighting me with everything she had in her. Didn't she know what kind of danger she was in?

"You're scared too, aren't you?" Hannah continued in a low, comforting tone. "Here I thought you had this master plan, and you've just been winging it the whole time. Man, this shit is scary." Her voice trembled a bit, and my heart rate slowed down as I realized how brave she was. Docile didn't come naturally to Hannah. At all.

I buried my face in her neck, inhaling the scent of her. Of campfires and fall leaves, the same color as her hair. The smell of outdoors and the wind and . . . something else. There was a new smell to her in that moment. Something gentle and sweet—acceptance. That's what we needed—both myself and the beast inside me. Our mate's acceptance. And while it wasn't solid enough to complete the mate bond, to fix all the broken things, it went miles to ease the burning ache inside me, the need to take and to punish. Her gentle caresses on my shoulders and back soothed my angry animal, and he was content to retreat for a moment.

I inhaled that sweet scent again, placing what I hoped was a chaste kiss on the skin between her neck and shoulder. That patch of skin that was exposed because of our tumble into the dirt, and her plaid button-down shirt was all askew, the collar open wide and inviting. Neither of us had put a jacket on in our wild haste to get out of town. I didn't feel cold. *I wonder if she's uncomfortable?*

Funny how I had her pressed into the dirt hard enough to leave a body print and my main concern as her mate was whether she experienced discomfort.

"Are you well enough to pick now?"

"Huh?" Her words floated up to me and broke through my idle thoughts.

Hannah squirmed underneath me, and her fingers plucked at the back of my shirt absently, like they had a mind of their own. I didn't hate it.

"Well, you seem to have calmed down a little, and your eyes are brown again instead of that crazy silver-white color. And your boner isn't digging a hole in my thigh anymore, so I thought maybe you were cool now. So about the sex or shift thing—are you in control? Can you pick which one you want now?"

Both I and my beast perked up at her shy request. Did that mean she was curious about us?

"Do you want to see me?"

She smiled, and for a moment I forgot where we were and what we were doing as the simple joy on her face outshone the drama of our situation.

"I really would."

"Close your eyes." I picked myself up off the ground, bringing Hannah with me. I carefully brushed the loose dirt from her clothes, wincing as I saw the third and fourth button of her shirt had been torn off. She saw me looking and smoothed her hands down the front, a blush staining her cheeks.

"Don't worry about it right now. We're focusing on something else. Now why do I have to close my eyes?"

"Because I have to get naked to shift, and I don't want you to get distracted by my naked body."

Hannah laughed so hard she snorted. "Oh please. I have more self-control than that."

"Well, I don't. Sex or shift, right? You picked shift, so close your eyes, because if you think I won't get an erection from you staring at my naked body then go ahead, keep looking. We can always change your mind." I was only half kidding, but she turned around and squeezed her eyes shut anyway. I tried not to let her hear me laughing as I shucked my clothes as quickly as I could.

We were both ready for the change—both my beast and me. Internally, I referred to him as a separate entity, an entirely different consciousness, but in reality, we were just two sides of the same being, existing in the same shell. I was him and he was me. Beast was man and man was beast. The change came quickly. Sometimes it didn't, but in this instance, the relief of our mate's acceptance was so monumental that my skin flowed to feathers and wings burst forth in one fluid motion.

Sometimes it was painful and messy. This was a religious experience.

I couldn't speak in my beast form, so I couldn't tell Hannah when to turn around and open her eyes, but she instinctively seemed to know. The flash of lightning and the answering roll of thunder were the only form of communication I could offer, and I used them to get her attention. Because that was in my control, the power I called to myself. Once worshipped as a deity of thunder, I commanded the skies.

Look at me, mate. Crack. Boom. The skies commanded, and Hannah turned, eyes wide and staring, mouth hanging open. We preened, spreading our silvery white wings tipped in shades of smoke gray and midnight blue. We couldn't fly in the cramped clearing with the low-hanging branches due to our sheer size, but we wanted to look our best anyway. For our mate. Would she think us impressive? It was really important.

"Oh my god, you're beautiful," Hannah whispered, showing no

fear as she approached. We stood as still as possible so as not to spook her. Would she come close enough to touch us? "And you're huge."

We were very proud of our stature and size. Our mate's words pleased us. We moved a bit, careful not to catch Hannah with our claws, which were easily the size of her head. We wouldn't harm her, never, but we couldn't be too careful during the exploratory phase.

Lightning zipped across the sky, a quick merry chase into the clouds to show our happiness. Hannah looked up and froze.

"I know what you are," she whispered, all cockiness gone as awe spread across her face and she worshipped us with her words. "Great-Granny River used to talk about you every time it stormed outside. She had wooden figurines on her mantel Dade and I used to play with when we were little." Hannah's chin trembled as she reached out to touch above our razor-sharp beak. Her hand shook as she let just the tips of her fingers graze the short bristly feathers there.

The thunder boomed, a joyful sound.

"Thunder Brother, what mischief are you up to, I wonder?" We don't think she meant to say the words out loud. They sounded like a repetition of something someone else had said—possibly this Great-Granny River? But as soon as the words were out of her mouth, her hands flew to cover it, and she dropped to her knees in the dirt, mouth open in shock.

"Holy shit, Chevy. You aren't just a shifter. You're a thunderbird. You're a fucking *god*."

Immediately we pulled back into our skin. Wings tucked in tight against our body, feathers gave way to flesh until I stood there, naked above her. I knelt next to her in the dirt that was slowly turning to mud with the gentle rain that fell down around our shoulders. For any other person, reverence was a good thing. As the descendent of a deity it was only fitting. But not Hannah. I reached under her chin and lifted it until she was looking at me. I wasn't a god, only the offspring of a spirit who once was.

"It makes my heart glad that you know me, even if just a little bit." I poured every bit of truth into my words I could. "I'm a thunderbird, a descendent of kings, ruler of the skies. Anyone else can kneel, but you are my mate, Hannah. You kneel for no one. And you were only half right. My ancestors were originally gods, but gods only exist when there are people to worship them. My kind faced extinction from lack of prayers and left the heavens to take human bodies long before my time. That's how we're different from other shifters. So get off your knees, babe. I'm not a god. I'm a descendent of one. Just like you."

I kissed her. Not a hard kiss this time, but a gentle kiss. A greeting from her mate, whom she had now seen in entirety. The acceptance was still there, a sweet scent on the breeze, but still not enough to solidify the mate bond. We would need to join physically again for that, and I knew without words that she was still too afraid, too uncertain. I had more to say, more information to tell her that would be too much to handle right now. And I didn't have a lot of time to get my point across, but she deserved to know. The truth of our kind. The truth of my people. And may she still choose me after I told her everything I had to say.

CHAPTER 8

HANNAH

I'd barely closed my eyes to sleep when a pressure at the foot of my bed snapped my eyelids open like window shades, and I bolted upright in bed. Chevy and I had spent hours sitting in the dark of the forest talking, and he had unloaded some seriously heavy shit on me.

Was it too much to ask for a couple hours of quality sleep to process the information? My brother Dade thought so. His mop of curly hair hung over his brown eyes, but that dopey grin was there in full effect. I could tell by the look on his face which of his three souls had the wheel today, and a quick glance at his butt, hovering two inches above the mattress he had just bounced off of, sealed the deal. Dade was going to be a handful this morning. Oh joy.

"Care to explain why you crawled into the apartment at oh dark thirty covered in mud and missing three buttons off your shirt?" He tried to sound like a concerned parent, but I could hear the laughter in his voice. "Rough night?"

"You have no idea," I groaned, and flung the covers off the bed. I flung them at Dade, actually, but he just floated a few feet over to the right, and the blankets completely missed him. He didn't even change positions, just floated in a half lounge, arms crossed behind his head and completely supported by the surrounding air.

"It's been twenty-six years since my family adopted you, and it still weirds me out when you do that."

Dade's expression sobered instantly. "Sorry."

His face fell, and I was immediately apologetic for saying anything. He dropped like a stone to a standing position, his bare feet firm on the short beige carpeting of my bedroom floor.

"No, Dade, I'm sorry. I'm just sleep-deprived and grumpy and . . . overwhelmed."

"Scared."

Yeah, I forgot about that too. This Dade was an empath. He could feel what I was feeling. Make me feel more of it too, if he had a bug up his ass about something. Hopefully today was not one of those days, but at least one thing was certain: I could not lie to Dade about what I was feeling. Not when he was in this soul cycle.

"Can't fib with me on this one, Hannah." Dade sat next to me on the bed, on the actual mattress this time, and pulled me into a familiar side hug. "He's kind of a big deal, isn't he?"

Tears pricked the back of my eyelids, and I squeezed them closed to keep any water from falling. I'd told Chevy to give me the day for space—we'd talked about so many things. So many overwhelming things. Even though I was the one who asked for space, as soon as I opened my eyes this morning, I felt the loss. My whole soul was screaming for my mate.

I had some huge decisions to make.

Dade fell backwards onto the covers and spread his arms and legs out like he was making a blanket angel, almost knocking me completely off the side of the bed before putting his arms behind his head and looking up at the ceiling with a small smile on his face.

"Hey, what are you doing, bed hog?" We hadn't lain in the same bed together since we were kids. Since long before Mom and Dad moved away from Havenwood Falls. But I remembered a time when we were as close as two siblings could be. Sometimes, when the soul cycle was too much for Dade to bear, he would crawl into my bed, curl up in a ball and shake. No tears, because big boys didn't cry, at least not that their sisters acknowledged. There was no one in the world quite like Dade, even in Havenwood Falls. As the older sibling, it was my job to protect him. Somehow, in the last ten years or so, he'd grown up on me.

"When you leave, I'm taking your room."

His words hit me like a punch to the gut, and for a moment I was so shocked I couldn't respond. He didn't look over at me, didn't register my jaw going slack or my eyes glossing over. Chevy had mentioned it, yeah. He'd explained the events surrounding mate suppression, the experiments, and what he'd been trying to do since he left the compound. And I'd thought it over, sure. But I hadn't actually considered leaving Havenwood Falls. I mean, we really needed to have more discussion about this first. Chevy and me.

I couldn't leave Dade. He needed me. Three souls, all with different abilities, all inhabiting one body—a chimera of sorts. Physically one person, emotionally he was something else. We don't know if he was born that way. We don't know if someone made him that way using magic. We only know that the Court came to my parents when I was young and asked them to foster a special child. My mother was human, and my father's blood just diluted enough to pass on the recessive genes of both Granny River and Papa Jonas, but they both knew what it was like to have a special child. Growing up, Dade was difficult for everyone, but I loved my little brother from the first day he came to our home. No matter which soul was in possession of the body at any given time. But Dade had special needs.

And Dade could never leave Havenwood Falls. The tattoo on his arm helped regulate the inconsistencies in his personalities better than any medication, but it wouldn't work outside of the wards for long. So no, Dade would never go outside the wards for any real length of time, but here he was talking about me leaving like it was the only logical option. I'd never thought of it. Not once.

I couldn't breathe. Dade continued to look at the ceiling, that silly smile on his face, and I continued to blink rapidly, determined not to let the tears fall. *Don't call me out like this. I'm not ready.*

"I can feel your fear and your sadness, Hannah. But you know what exists underneath all of that?" Dade turned his head to look at me then, his dark puppy eyes searching my face for the answer to the questions he really didn't need answers to. He was trying to make a point. "I can feel him. Your connection to him. Your need. That was never there before. It's new." He shuddered and looked away, like he saw something in me that pained him. "It hurts you, doesn't it? Being away from him? You can't keep it up for much longer."

"How do you know any of this? I haven't said a thing. Don't go kicking me out of the apartment because you got a feeling." I was snappy. I was defensive. He saw right through it immediately, because he was Dade and of course he did. "I just met him two days ago."

"Yeah, I know. I was at the bar with you when you kidnapped him and made him leave with you." Dade laughed and sat up on the bed next to me. "You can blame him and his weird smells all you want, but I was there. You threw yourself at him, Hannah. And I was here yesterday when he came to see you in the studio. You are not very good at the quiet game."

Oh God, he'd heard us?

"Dade, I'm so sorry." I couldn't even begin to apologize for how uncomfortable my actions must have made him. For making him question my devotion to him as a sister, for making him feel uncertain about his place. I would always be here to take care of Dade. Always.

"I don't need you to take care of me."

"Yeah, I know." We'd had this talk before. Dade was grown, but he'd always be my little brother with special needs. He did okay day to day, but all it would take was one wrong move in front of an unsuspecting human and then what? Outside they would diagnose Dade as split personality, or maybe a form of schizophrenia, but they'd be so wrong. I needed to keep an eye on Dade, to protect him from people who would harm him, thinking they were "doing the right thing."

Dade sighed, and I tried not to take it personally, but he was losing patience with me. "Hannah, I'm an adult. Did you know that? We can't share an apartment for the rest of our lives, you know. At some point I'm going to want to have crazy kinky sex with someone too. Who knows, maybe I'll get a girlfriend. Or a boyfriend. Maybe both?"

I laid my odds on both. He could crack jokes all he wanted. Dade didn't bring men or women home—he got up to his freaky stuff at Silk. We had a pretty good policy at home. We didn't bring our partners to the apartment. That was our space.

"I've never heard you say anything about wanting a boyfriend or girlfriend, Dade. I didn't think you ever thought of it."

"No, *you* never thought of it for *yourself*. You don't know what I think about. You don't ask." Was—was he angry? It was hard to tell with that wistful smile on his face, but I thought I detected a tightness in his voice.

"Dade. I'm not leaving you, okay? So, you don't have to act like this. It's okay—"

"Yeah, it *is* okay. Hannah, you're the only one who doesn't seem to get it. This thing with that Walker guy? It's bigger than you think it is. You're a part of something huge, the missing biological key that goes back in your bloodline. Don't you want to know more about that? Hell, even Great-Granny River would have given anything to learn more about herself. You don't know who you are. You don't know where your powers came from. But there could be other people like you out there, outside of Havenwood Falls. Don't you want to know? You won't learn about it here."

I did. I wanted to so badly. If what Chevy said was true, and everything he had told me until this point was, then there were countless other people out there like me. Descendants of old gods, carriers of divine blood. Mate suppression was a science experiment, and Chevy and his friends were lab rats. Growing up in a cult environment, not knowing about the other person they were connected to out in the world. Chemical suppression, all for the sake of breeding—of keeping the bloodline pure. It made me sick. Of course I wanted to know. But knowing meant leaving, and leaving meant countless other painful things.

Equivalent exchange. The alchemy of Havenwood Falls. There is no gain without loss. I couldn't gain that knowledge or that freedom without losing something very precious. I should know—my parents paid that price when they left too.

"I can't take you with me." If it hurt to think it, the pain was a hundred times worse when I said the words out loud. Dade may have had a smile on his face—*that fucking smile*—but his eyes held every other emotion.

"You sure can't. We both know I can't exist outside of Havenwood Falls, Hannah. For all its faults and shortcomings, this town exists for people like me. I'm safe here. People are safe from me here. I'm good."

Then why do you sound so sad?

"I think you'll be fine no matter where you go, and there's no denying your connection to Chevy Walker. I can feel your bond without even trying. And I'm not saying you need to leave Havenwood Falls. Hell, Chevy might be better off staying here instead. I just want you to think about the possibilities. For someone so hung up on not losing your powers to some man, you sure didn't pay attention to any of the rest of the stuff Granny River had to teach us."

"What are you talking about?" I remembered more of Granny River than he did.

Dade cleared his throat, hopped up from the bed and tapped an imaginary microphone in front of him. "Testing. Is this thing on? Let me tell you a story, Hannah, about when the world was new, and the gods still ruled the sky."

Oh geez, not these old stories again. I rolled my eyes, but he kept talking, pacing in front of the bed and making grand gestures with his hands because amongst other things, Dade had a flair for the dramatic.

"Many years ago, when the old gods still came to the earth to bless the people, a firebird passed through the Western lands from the East, on his way to sing to the sun. He saw a beautiful woman, and taking the form of a man, made her his wife. He lived that way for many years, but after she returned to the earth from which she came, the firebird shed his human form, took wing again, and left the Western lands. During his time, however, he'd fathered a single daughter, and thus began the legend of the original fire maiden."

"I remember these old stories, but what does that have to do with me?"

"At some point, the people of the land became afraid. The fire maidens possessed unimaginable power themselves, but their power was from a foreign land. A foreign god. So as not to anger the gods of this land, the fire maidens were treated as chattel. Living a life of slavery until they could be used as a bargaining chip to gain position and dominance over other tribes. Once a sign of great power and nobility, the birth of a fire maiden became a sign of calamity, and more than likely, if found, were put to death."

"Dade. I know the stories of how the fire maidens were treated. Granny River told us about it when she told us about going to that school when she was a child. It was extra hard for her trying to stay hidden from her own tribe and then keeping it from her teachers. But that's all there is to the backstory. And it was just a story Granny told, handed down from her people. It wasn't real."

Dade stopped his pacing and flung his hands in the air, disappointment stamped on his face. "I wish you would listen when people talk instead of fabricating things in your mind. I'm saying, what if you're the child of a firebird? What if that's where your flames came from? You're a direct descendant of a god, Hannah. Get your head out of your ass."

"The firebird is a Slavic myth, Dade. So you're saying a foreign bird god went on a trip, found a pretty piece of ass, hung out for a bit, and then jetted after having a baby?" Actually saying it out loud sounded like every mythological god story ever created.

"I'm saying think about it, Hannah. And up until two days ago, the thunder brothers were just a myth too, weren't they?"

Okay, now I was really confused. I just found out about Chevy's heritage last night. How was Dade even hinting at knowing what

Chevy was? The question must have shown on my face, because Dade laughed.

"You talk in your sleep, Hannah. Always have."

I swatted his arm, my mind reeling with the point he was trying to make. Chevy said that being a descendant of a god did not make you a mate, but all mates were descendants of gods. It was a plausible theory that had never occurred to me before, and it took Dade rubbing my own family history in my face to even think about it.

"Why do you remember this stuff and I don't?"

Dade plopped down on the bed next to me again, his long legs stretching out farther than mine and crossing at the ankles as he leaned his head on my shoulder. His curly hair tickled my nose, and I sneezed.

"Because, sis, I don't have a family history. For all I know, I could be a test tube baby. No one in the Court will tell me when I ask, and there are no birth records at the hospitals. I can't ask Mom and Dad, because they're long gone. And here you are, sitting amidst a wealth of knowledge if you'd just do a little digging. What are you so afraid of? I've always wanted to know."

"Granny River lost her power to a man, Dade. You know that. She fell in love with Jonas and let a vampire seal her power away. I'll never let anyone do that to me. Never." I don't know why I even had to explain it again. Dade knew exactly how I felt about it. We'd been over this many times. It's the reason I didn't date. Didn't do relationships. The reason I didn't want to be a mate. No man would take my identity away from me. I wasn't Granny River. I would fight to keep what was mine.

"I don't think you're thinking of the same story, Hannah. From what I understand, that power got sealed away for her protection, and she wasn't too broken up to see it go. I think you're dwelling too much on something that doesn't even exist. Has Chevy ever mentioned taking your power when you're mated?"

"No." Not yet. It hadn't actually come up, considering every time we were near each other, the mate bond went bananas and it was sex sex sex.

"Then maybe that's something that would never happen. Have you tried talking with him about it?"

"No." Again, not yet. Even thinking about the conversation was aggravating. My skin was hot and prickly, and my eyelids scratched like sandpaper over my tired eyes.

"You're thinking about him right now, aren't you? Your fingernails are leaving marks on your palms. Damn, girl, you've got it bad." Dade's voice sounded far away, and I rubbed my eyes to make sure he was still sitting next to me.

My mind was a mess. I wanted Chevy, but I didn't want to lose my identity or my power. My body screamed for him, and my heart echoed the sentiment, but my mind was still angry and confused. Would he try to take my power away like Gabe and Jonas had done to River? I would have loved to pick Jonas's brain about it, but he was long gone. And Gabe was less than forthcoming with the information. He'd be a lot more trustworthy source if he would just return the amulet, but he never would, no matter how many times I asked. Begged. Threatened even.

And the tears I'd been holding back spilled over then, a bitter stream running down my cheeks.

"I don't want to talk about this right now, okay?" And I didn't. Because my brother was giving me sound advice that I really didn't want to hear. And if I was awake, I would just think about Chevy, and when I thought about Chevy, I completely lost my mind and self-control. "I just need to get some sleep. It will be easier to think once I get some good rest."

Dade left me alone then, without another hug or any other words of comfort. I didn't have any for him either. The reality of the situation was everything changed for all of us when Chevy Walker came to town. He might not have known the impact he was going to have, but that didn't change his role. I'd have a good cry and get some sleep, then I would make him take responsibility.

CHAPTER 9

CHEVY

I promised I'd give her at least the day before I went to her again. I could adhere to that agreement, couldn't I? Physically yes, but emotionally I was all over the place.

She was right across the fucking street. If I opened the window and yelled, I could get her to answer me. But what good would that do? What Hannah needed was a partner she could trust, regardless of how the biology of mates worked. She had some serious hang-ups to work through before she committed, and if I couldn't do this one simple thing . . .

But my body burned. My animal kept me from going crazy, but Hannah didn't have an animal. How was she handling the stress? It couldn't be sheer stubbornness holding her back, could it? Considering what I knew of Hannah, maybe it could. Maybe females were less susceptible to the mate sickness than males were. I wished there was more information. Unfortunately, I was patient zero in this equation. Any information regarding the mate bond for thunderbirds would come from me.

Hats off to the guinea pig.

I'd told Hannah I needed sex or a shift, but the shift was just a natural response to the excruciating amount of stress I was under. This perma-hard-on I was sporting would not go away until the mate bond was satisfied, and the mate bond required lots of sex. I didn't need a dusty old book to tell me that. My body was screaming it loud and clear, and a one-night stand and a quick bend over Hannah's workbench were not enough to satisfy the need. Not by a long shot.

I should make notes. I should record my journey for the good of the caste, so when the truth was finally revealed, those newly awakened to the mate bond wouldn't suffer the same unknowing I did. It was easy for me to go through it. They had removed me from the family caste, thrown into the world as a defect.

They'd thought it was a punishment. I'd never felt more liberated. I don't know what strings Baz pulled to get the other elders to let go of me. Maybe he'd fudged some blood tests. Maybe he'd told them I was impotent. I don't know, but both scenarios were highly likely. Bloodline purity was of the utmost importance to the thunderbird line. But fuck their master plan of playing hide and go seek with the truth. Fuck their generations of drugged suppression, teaching everyone the medicine is necessary for righting the weaknesses in our DNA. They were fucking with our genetic code. *And for what?* Purity? Our species was dying out, and they still had everyone fooled into thinking it was the only way. Even if Baz and I were the only ones who knew right now—we were starting a revolution. All of those thunderbird shifters matched by the elders because "it was the best way to breed." Did we have the fertility problems the elders would have us believe? Or was it *because* we weren't allowed to match with our actual mates that we had seen the decline of our kind?

They'd even go so far as to drug the entire caste to perpetuate the species. Even commit genocide. We weren't an elite shifter species anymore. We were a damn cult. And I would do my best to free everyone from the spell.

If the elders knew about Hannah and me, they'd eliminate her. And me as well, making me a lesson to the rest of the family about what happens when you try to buck the system. Or maybe they'd cover it up like we never existed. Either was reprehensible. My body would go cold in the ground before anyone touched my mate. And even after death, they'd have a fight on their hands.

Hannah.

Even saying her name inside my head caused a chain reaction throughout my entire body. Sparks shot across my nerve endings, and my skin crawled with need. *Release.* I had to have it.

My cock was so swollen just at the thought of Hannah. The mate bond would overpower me. I'd run across the street and pin her to the floor, maul her like an animal no matter who was watching. I knew it. It would be hot and violent. She would scent me and respond. She would drip for me, I knew it.

But she would never forgive me.

And I needed that. I needed that trust from my mate. I needed to never see her cry because I hurt her. Because I forced my need on her. Even though I knew her need was just as great, a mate wasn't a quick fuck. A mate was forever, and the bond demanded acceptance. A truth that wasn't written in that ratty old memoir, but something my body knew instinctively.

She had to accept me on a spiritual level, or the need would get stronger. Nothing would change until we came together of the same mind, and if that didn't happen, the cycle would continue, over and over until it destroyed us both.

A cold shower would help, but that wasn't what was on my mind as I turned on the water, the setting almost as hot as it would go. My body didn't want to calm down; what I needed was a release. Well, what I needed was to sink down between Hannah's soft thighs but since I promised her time to think, my options were limited.

The hot shower felt damn good, and the water pressure was just firm enough that the spray pelted the skin on my back and thighs, the water running in a steamy river down my chest and abdomen. My erection surged upwards, solid and heavy against my belly, aching to be touched. She was just across the street. So close. I may have been forbidden from seeing her, but she couldn't stop me from thinking about her.

Her face appeared behind my closed eyes as I poured liquid soap over my hands and between my fingers until they were nice and slippery. Her amber eyes, those pupils just pinholes expanding and contracting when she first caught my scent. That moment of awareness when she grabbed my arm and dragged me out of the bar when we first met.

Hell yes, I'd think about her.

That mouth of hers. The same mouth she used to curse me she'd had wrapped so tightly around my cock not two days before. That's what I wanted to think about as my soapy hands slicked over my balls. As my fingers gripped tightly and stroked, slipping lightly against my sensitive flesh.

I remembered what she tasted like too. That sweet pussy with the tidy patch of hair, the same fiery color as the locks on her head, just slightly darker. She'd been just as greedy with my mouth as I'd been with hers, locking her legs behind my neck and squeezing her thighs tight so I had no choice but to stay there, to suck her more fully into my mouth. That was our first time together. But there were more.

My strokes weren't so gentle anymore. No, I thrust into my hand like I'd thrust into Hannah from behind, hips bucking in much the same way as when I'd bent her over her workbench. Her halfhearted struggle completely at odds with the wetness I found when my hand touched her heat. She'd been dripping, all but begging me to take her even as her mind rallied against the idea of being my mate. All I was missing was the slap of our skin and her low moans as she tried so hard to keep from making any noise. I wanted her to make more noise.

I wanted Hannah to scream.

And I knew she would, because as much as she argued about it, Hannah liked it rough. She liked my hand on her neck, holding her in place while I brought her to the brink. I wouldn't do it if she didn't like it, but the first time she put my hands where she wanted them, I knew. Hannah needed someone to control her. Her body wouldn't lie even if her mind tried to.

Next time, I'd tie her hands and see how she reacted.

That exact image sprang to mind—Hannah, naked and

kneeling, her hands tied behind her back, mouth slightly parted with curiosity. So many things I wanted to do with Hannah, if I could just give her one fucking day.

Fuck, that water felt so good coursing over my body as I punished my cock with those thoughts, stroking harder and faster to match the rhythm of my mind. Hannah's hair messy and wild as she rode me, her tits bouncing up and down.

Oh God. The smooth globes of her ass as I bent her over and took her from behind, my fingers stroking her clit as I tortured her with long, smooth strokes. Long and smooth was just my imagination though. My hand movements were far fiercer as I tugged hard on my aching dick and squeezed with one hand, the other sliding over and around my sensitive sack.

The tremors started in my legs, but I ignored them, chasing my prize. Visions of Hannah exploded behind my eyes like starbursts as I pumped fast and hard, the sound of soap squelching against my skin lost under the thunder of the hot water spray. Shuddering, I lost my load against the shower wall, my groan of release echoing off the wet tiles.

Was it perverse, jerking off to my memories of Hannah while she struggled with her own demons not more than a few dozen meters away? Maybe, but I didn't have a choice. The mate bond would not be denied, and there was only one way to make it better. I'd give her one day. That was all my patience—and the mate bond—would allow.

In no hurry to leave the warmth of the shower, I stood under the spray with my eyes closed, letting the water run down my face and neck. There was no way to know how many more times I would go through this before the day was over. The mate bond did not know fatigue, and even though I was spent, just thinking about Hannah caused my body to thicken in response. Fuck it. I'd stay in the shower until I was a prune, or until I could say Hannah's name without getting an immediate, raging erection.

Hurry and decide, mate. My control was slipping.

CHAPTER 10

HANNAH

I know I told Chevy to give me some time, but I was already feeling the stress of being away from him. The mate bond pulled tightly, making me feel woozy and slightly nauseous the longer I was away. But even though I was pretty solid in my decision to join him, to make our mating permanent and leave Havenwood Falls, there was still something I needed to do before I said goodbye. Before I left my friends and my memories behind.

I had to go see Uncle Gabe.

More precisely, I had to retrieve something from Uncle Gabe, and that something was my great-grandmother's amulet. The one that sealed her powers almost a hundred years ago. I think I could face Chevy with a fresh outlook if I could just get that back. If I could prove that something stolen from her wasn't lost forever. It was the last thing I needed to do before accepting my role—before accepting Chevy Walker as my mate. Even thinking about him in passing brought fresh waves of heat rippling through my body. In the beginning, it was a wonderful feeling, brimming with desire. Now I was just sick, and the waves that spontaneously rolled through my body were nausea, not pleasure. The mate bond was still there, but it was sick and sticky. Something wasn't right, but I still had something to do before I could find Chevy and ask him about it. Before I could try to fix it.

I'd been friends with Alina since she came to town a few months ago, but I hated visiting the house she shared with Gabe. The house that was formerly, and now again, home to the newly revamped Lilith Nest of vampires. It looked it too, sitting on the edge of town with its Gothic architecture and dark colors. That was just the outside. The inside was just as ornately decorated, with spindly-legged furniture that screamed aristocracy. I was afraid to sit on anything in that house, which was why I always met Alina somewhere else. I loved her. I hated that house.

But there I was anyway, perched on a settee that I imagined cost more than my entire store and was probably more antique than my Aunties McNee, holding a hot cup of tea and wondering how to even get started on what I wanted to say. Gabe sat next to Alina on a two-seater across from me, his eyebrow arched expectantly. He knew what I wanted, I was sure. I'd only been pestering him for it since he came back to Havenwood Falls and I found out he was the same Gabe from Granny River's stories.

She'd painted him as a savior. I knew him as a villain. Why else would he be hanging on to my grandmother's power? It should be with her family. It belonged with me, and I would take it back.

But first I had to say the words, and they were so difficult to spit out with my best friend sitting across from me, and her dusty vampire boyfriend smirking at me over the rim of my steaming cup of Earl Grey.

"Do you guys sit in this room often?" I looked around at the incredibly bougie interior. I couldn't imagine kicking back and watching a movie here on a Friday night. There wasn't even an entertainment center. Or a television. I wondered if anyone had ever spilled a drink or bowl of popcorn in here, and what sort of death penalty awaited them because of it.

"Your mind is fascinating as always, Hannah. You look like you're ready to bolt. Care to spit out what is creating that sour look on your face?" Gabe drawled from his position next to Alina, voice dripping with polite sarcasm and mouth quirking up at the corners. That was another thing I hated about Gabe. How he talked like he was so superior to everyone else. And his ability to read my mind. So damn frustrating. Alina grinned next to him. Apparently, she was his girlfriend first, my best friend second.

Traitor. I sent her a glare. She stuck her tongue out at me in response.

"I'm here to retrieve what belongs to my family, Uncle Gabe." I used the pet name like a weapon, knowing how badly it got under his skin. He was no uncle of mine. Not in blood or in spirit. "My life is growing increasingly complicated, and right now my only option is to follow my mate." I took a deep breath as emotion clogged my throat. "I wanted to come and talk to Alina. I want to ask you to take care of Dade, okay? He's an idiot who needs constant supervision. He's a good glass teacher, you know that, but his social skills need some serious work. So don't leave him alone, okay? I need to know he's going to be all right."

Damnit, every word was true. I could tell myself I just came for Granny's amulet, but I really, desperately needed to know someone was looking out for Dade. And who better to trust my brother with than my best friend? The shop would be in good hands with the two of them. But my brother needed the *best* hands.

I hadn't planned on crying. I really hadn't. But that mate bond caused some serious emotional distress, so pretty much all it took was a commercial for baby wipes and I was ready to burst into tears. I don't know how I thought I was going to get through a goodbye without dissolving into hiccupping sobs.

Alina was on her feet and next to me in a moment, her long dark hair falling over my shoulders as she crushed me into the kind of hug only best friends can give.

"Dade is a man, Hannah. You're acting like you're leaving Havenwood Falls. You don't even know what's going to happen tomorrow, so why are you planning on leaving?" She patted my hair in an attempt to soothe me, and I sniffled in response. So much for being brave and keeping my composure. My vision swam a bit, and I recognized the feeling. I'd been away from Chevy too long. I needed to complete my mission and get back to him or I'd probably turn into an emotionally drunk sex maniac. Gabriel stifled a laugh with his hand.

"Stay out of my head, you pervert."

"Stop shouting your thoughts at me, you brat. Trust me, it's not my preference." The older vampire's eyes snapped an icy blue warning, and I remembered. He may be my best friend's lover, but he was no ally of mine.

"Guys, don't fight. It stresses me out." Alina interrupted us with her mothering words. "Hannah, you have to do what is right for you. You know I'll always watch out for Dade and the shop, but I think you are underestimating him a little. And Chevy too. If he's as important as he seems to be, and I've never seen you fritz out over a guy before, then maybe you should give him a little more credit. And while you're at it, give Dade some credit too. Geez, you make him sound like a child."

Dade was more special than most people realized. He could never exist outside of Havenwood Falls. That's why I stayed. When my parents moved away, I had no choice but to stay with him and take care of him. Dad took a job in Missouri when I was twenty-two and Dade was seventeen. They knew their memories would be lost after they left, but we all made peace with that. That's how life was in Havenwood Falls—and out of it. It's the price we paid for our safety, and our way of life. We all knew that, but it didn't make things easier for any of us.

It was heartbreaking to say goodbye to your parents, knowing it was the last time you would see them as they smiled and drove away. One month after they left was the last time I heard from either of them. I had their last known address. Maybe when I left I could . . .

No. When I left, I would lose my memories in the same amount of time. Neither Chevy nor I would retain any of our memories of Havenwood Falls—the place nor the people. But that was how important his situation was. He was my mate, and he needed me—

needed me—so I would go. But I would take my grandmother's pendant with me.

I deserved that.

"What makes you think I would give you that amulet? That it would belong to you in any way?"

Once again intruding on my private thoughts, Gabe butted in. My sadness immediately turned to anger. That was the effect he had on me.

"Oh boy," Alina muttered under her breath, throwing her hands in the air and rising to her feet. Pacing the space between where Gabe and I sat, she grumbled. "Must everything between you two be an argument?"

"*Must* Gabriel think he is superior to everyone and the world's populace exists to serve him?"

"*Must* you be a spoiled brat who has never experienced real struggle or even stepped foot outside the protective circle of your precious little town? A young girl with zero life experience and serious entitlement issues thinks to judge me on my attitude? Grow up, little girl. Real life is not so pleasant. Existence is pain. You are a hundred years too young to judge me on anything."

Red rage spilled over me, and nausea twisted my guts in knots. Heat flushed my body from head to toe, and I had to bite my tongue to keep from lashing out. Not with words, but with my flames.

This guy . . .

"Hannah, you don't look so good." Alina probably meant well, but I was tired of people telling me I didn't look well. That I needed a rest. That I needed to let go. This was personal, I had shit to do, and I wasn't leaving Havenwood Falls without tying up all the loose ends.

"Butt out, Alina. If you aren't helping, you're hindering." My voice sounded different. Thicker, strained. I didn't know why, but it was becoming difficult to speak. Small wisps of orange hair floated in front of my eyes. Strange that there was a breeze inside, and such a warm one too. The air crackled with energy, but it didn't bother me. Nope. It felt pretty damned good.

"Give me my grandmother's necklace, and you'll never see me again." There. I said the words.

"Absolutely not. It isn't meant for you."

"What do you want from me? Money? Will it take money to buy back my family's legacy from you?" I tasted the bile, thick and acidic in my mouth. The thought of paying for my grandmother's necklace was disgusting to me, but people like Gabriel Doyle only thought about one thing. Money and power. I didn't have either of those things but was not above bluffing to get what I wanted.

"There is nothing you have that I could want, little girl," Gabe said, never moving from his seated position, which infuriated me all the more. There were sparks in front of my vision. Little bits of ash and flame dancing in front of my eyes. It delighted me, because the fire was mine. That was my power, just like it had been Granny River's, and even though she had lost hers by falling in love with a man, I had full control of mine. I'd never let anyone, mate or not, take that away from me.

"Ah, there it is. That's what you're really afraid of, isn't it? That by accepting your mate and accepting his love that you'll lose the thing most precious to you? That's your concern? That's why you're so bent about taking the amulet from me?"

"Get out of my head." I screamed the words at him. Flung them across the room, more like. Gabe stood this time, but not trying to get away from me or the heat waves radiating from my body. No, he was coming closer. That lunatic wasn't afraid of me. He wasn't afraid of anybody. But he should have been. My blood was boiling over, and the control I had on my power was a lid about to blow. When it did, Gabriel Doyle did not want to be in front of me.

"Hannah, please stop. I know you don't want to hurt anybody." But I didn't want to hear Alina pleading with me, and I turned toward her, hissing my rage and sending little tendrils of smoke and ash spitting in her direction.

"The right to wave your power around ends where my lover

stands," Gabriel interrupted coldly, commanding my attention again. My head hurt, my bones ached, and all I wanted to do was burn everything away. Take my grandmother's pendant and leave this town. My stomach hurt, and it took everything in me just to remain standing. But I wouldn't fall here. I would get what I came for.

"What do you know of what Jonas and River went through?"

"I grew up on those stories, vampire." Every word out of his mouth grated on my nerves.

"Was there something wrong with your ears then? Because if you'd been listening, you would know why your grandfather asked me for that amulet and why River willfully gave her power to it. That amulet saved her life. And fuck you for being a big, whiny baby about it."

It was rare for Gabe to show any emotion aside from sarcasm or boredom, so his words were an especially painful slap to the face.

"You are a bad man." Words failed me. That was the best I could do.

"You're right. I am a bad man, Hannah. I've never claimed to be otherwise. But let me tell you something. Jonas and River were *good* people. Genuinely good people, and for whatever reason, they both liked me, bad man that I am. But they are long gone, and here you are, a sorry excuse for a legacy. So I'm not going to let you stand there and piss all over everything they suffered just so you could exist on this earth. *Grow up*," Gabriel thundered at me. His voice actually rose enough to shake the walls, and I could hear footsteps running down corridors outside the room, but before any servants' hands could open the door, he spoke again.

"Do not enter this room."

The rattling of the doorknob stopped, but no footsteps retreated. They would obey, but they would also wait for the moment their master needed them. Such was the command of the leader of the Lilith Nest.

I wanted to light him on fire.

"River and Jonas would weep if they saw you now. That amulet

85

is mine to do with as I wish, and you are not deserving enough of such a gift. That necklace is not. Meant. For. You."

I wanted to throw up. Each word punched through me like a spear, hitting my body and flinging me back farther into the madness. Stumbling backward, I took one step to steady myself.

Then I exploded, focusing all of my rage, heat, and flames on Gabriel Doyle.

Alina screamed.

There was the shuffling of feet, the sharp sound of Alina chanting in a language I didn't understand, and then the snap of fingers and the world went dark.

Alina, the djinn that she was, shut me down and stole my consciousness.

Some friend she is. That was my last thought before the world turned inside out.

CHAPTER 11

CHEVY

I was going stir crazy waiting for Hannah to get her shit straight and come back, but even so, I was still taken aback by the knock on my hotel room door and the guy who could have been *Gotham*'s Alfred standing in the hallway waiting for me. He held a cell phone out without comment, and I could see the light on the screen showed a call was already live.

This was some Twilight Zone *stuff right here.*

"Hello?" Was it Hannah? We did exchange numbers before I dropped her off, so I don't know why I would be getting a cryptic call like this, but besides Addie and the staff at the inn, I hadn't really had any dealings with anyone else. Unless you counted that young punk Adrian, which I didn't.

The voice on the phone was definitely male, and definitely not Hannah.

"Mr. Walker." It wasn't a question. The smooth voice on the other end of the line was simply confirming what he already knew to be true and commanding my attention. That was an alpha personality tactic. I recognized it because I too had such a personality. The hairs stuck straight up on the back of my neck in warning.

"Where's Hannah?" I didn't know how I knew this was about

her. The mate bond, maybe. But if she wasn't calling me of her own volition, something wasn't right. Warning bells went off in my mind, and my beast reared his head, scenting the air for enemies.

"She's safe enough for now, although she's given us quite the hard time. My salon is a disaster, and she's currently confined to the lower floors for her own protection. This mate sickness is serious business, Mr. Walker. You should keep your woman on a tighter leash lest she cause problems for others."

There was no hint of malice in the stranger's voice. I was on my guard anyway. He had Hannah, and depending on what I had to do to get her back, he could be a friend or an enemy.

"Enzo will bring you to the house," the voice continued without waiting for me to reply. "Try to keep an open mind when you get here."

What the hell did that mean?

"Are you Enzo?" The dark-haired gentleman just nodded politely and turned and walked down the hallway, not waiting to see if I followed. I didn't bother to grab a jacket. I was afraid he would disappear on me, so I hauled ass down the stairs after him and jumped into the back of the shiny black Audi as he held the passenger door open for me.

It was an obnoxiously expensive car for a small town like Havenwood Falls, but I could still appreciate the craftsmanship. It wasn't that I couldn't afford one, but those flashy little cars didn't do so well off-roading in the desert. And for shifters with a wingspan like mine, the wide-open spaces were where we spent most of our time. Thinking of home reminded me of my purpose, my cause. I thought of all the people whose happiness and lives rested square on the success of my and Hannah's mating.

I didn't have long to contemplate my homecoming, as it was an embarrassingly short drive from Whisper Falls Inn on one side of Havenwood Falls to the towering gray Gothic mansion on the complete opposite side of town. It creeped me out that Enzo guy hadn't said one damn word the whole time, but maybe he was mute? It would probably be rude of me to ask.

My sense of impending danger only increased with the *Addams Family* vibe of the house, but the interior was remarkably modern compared to the outside. Wealth dripped from every fixture. You could tell the homeowner was a very fastidious person.

Or so I thought, until Enzo the Silent led me into an anterior parlor off the side of the entrance.

One two-seater sofa sat in pristine condition, and on it rested a dark-haired man with the most striking blue eyes I'd ever seen up close. I was pretty sure they were X-ray eyes, superhero eyes even. I'd have bet they could see right through me. The man's mouth quirked up at the corners after I had the thought, like he knew exactly what I was thinking.

Interesting.

"Thank you, Enzo."

"If that will be all, sir, I'll leave you to it."

Well, I'll be damned. Enzo could talk. And with a decidedly mild Italian accent too. I tried to make eye contact with him as he left the room, but he studiously ignored me and glided past without even a nod.

"Welcome to my home, Mr. Walker. My name is Gabriel Doyle. I would invite you to have a seat, but we are lacking in accommodations at the moment."

Underestimation of the century.

I tried not to let the shock show on my face, but that room was destroyed. The only untouched item in the room was the sofa Gabe sat on, and even the man himself looked to have been through the wringer, although his cool posture belied the shabby scorch marks on his shirt and the red, raised blisters on his neck and hands. They were well on the way to healing, but they weren't gone yet. The room had been torched. So had the man.

By Hannah.

Even without the burns everywhere, I would know it was her. Her scent was everywhere. I smelled her the minute I stepped foot in the door.

"Where is she?" It wasn't a question, but a demand for answers as the beast inside me reared his head in anger. Thunder boomed inside the small chamber, and my chest swelled with the need to change. To find Hannah. To rip this house to pieces and uncover where he'd hidden her. I would bring a storm of destruction into this building and blow the walls clean apart until she appeared before me.

To his credit, Gabriel didn't jump. Not even when lightning arced over his head and split the seat cushion in two right next to where he sat. It was a warning.

There wouldn't be another.

"I know who and what you are, so no need for the theatrics. I've lived lifetimes and traveled the world. I've seen more of your kind than you have. I get it. She's your mate." Gabriel stood, and the part of the sofa he'd been sitting on crumbled to pieces behind him. It had to have been holding him up with sheer willpower.

"Where is she?" I couldn't help but growl the question. A purely guttural sound. The mate bond was stretched impossibly thin. We needed to complete the bond soon, or no matter how my beast protected me, I would succumb to the madness too.

"That mate sickness is certainly a troubling condition," he said, ripping the words from my head and confirming my suspicion that he could read my thoughts. "Not my favorite pastime, I assure you. But reading minds does make things quicker sometimes, doesn't it?"

I did not like this guy.

"Most people don't." Gabe walked casually through the room, righting end tables and putting priceless knickknacks that hadn't been destroyed into dust back on their appropriate perches. Acting for all the world like a child who found a sibling had been in his room playing with his toys while he'd been gone.

A place for everything, and everything in its place.

"Hannah." Another one-word demand.

"She's *resting*." Gabriel gave me his full attention again. "She was a danger to herself and others. She had to be put to sleep."

"And just who put her to sleep?"

"I did." The female voice came from behind me, and I turned to see a stunning dark-haired beauty enter the room, her hair wild and tangled and her eyes red-rimmed and swollen. She'd been crying. A lot.

"Hannah is my friend. I would never hurt her, but she attacked Gabe. I couldn't let her . . ." The young woman burst into fresh tears, and Gabriel beckoned her forward.

"You didn't hurt her, love. You kept her from hurting anyone else." Gabriel pulled her close and pressed his lips to her hair as she sobbed into his destroyed shirt.

Several things became crystal clear in that moment. I knew who both of these people were, and I simultaneously became certain Hannah was in no danger from either of them.

"You're Alina, aren't you?"

She lifted her face to look at me and nodded.

"And I know you said your name was Gabriel, but it took me until just now to place you. You're the dusty vampire that stole Hannah's great-grandmother's amulet, right?"

"I remember it a little differently, but I suppose you're close," Gabe drawled, looking unamused. "Hannah has mentioned us, I see."

I looked at Gabriel again, noticing the marks on his body. He'd taken the brunt of her blast and hadn't bothered protecting himself. The scorch marks, partially healed blisters, and torn clothing didn't lie. He let her do it.

"They were your friends, weren't they? River and Jonas."

For the first time since I met him, Gabriel showed an emotion other than disdain. It was a surprise.

"Absurd. I don't have friends. I have servants and business associates. When you've lived as long as I have, human attachments become meaningless. Everything decays in the end." Alina put her arms around his waist and squeezed. "Ah, except my love for you," he amended and smiled when she blushed.

"Okay. I won't bust your balls about it. But tell me this. Do you love Hannah?"

"What is wrong with you? What in the hell kind of question is that?" Gabriel didn't just look uncomfortable with my line of questioning; he was downright scandalized. Terrified even. How dare I make him admit to having a feeling?

"She's like a daughter to you, or a favored niece even." If I kept talking, Gabe would vomit, I was sure of it. Even Alina had to hide her face in his shoulder to keep him from seeing her grin.

"Absolutely not. And watch your tongue or I will remove it from your mouth." He was serious.

It was hysterical.

"Okay. You don't love her. You don't even like her. You simply put her out of her own misery for personal protection. Where is she? Can I see her now?" My voice was calm and even, at complete odds with my beast, who was threatening to tear me apart from the inside out if I didn't lay my eyes, and hands, on her soon.

"I'll take you down to her, but I have to warn you. You're not going to like what you see. She's not in her right mind." Alina squared her shoulders and faced me defiantly, waiting to see if I would be aggressive with her.

What in the hell was going on?

"I think you know." Gabe was inside my head again. That was pretty annoying. "Everything you're feeling. All the pain of separation and anxiety you feel through the mate bond—it's in stereo for her. Whatever you need to do to become whole, do it soon. Otherwise she's going to self-destruct. And then you'll follow her."

The—*if something happens to her I'll kill you*—was left unspoken, but implied. I was getting a bead on our dusty old vampire, here. Bad guy indeed.

"Here, put this on if you want." I barely had time to lift my hand and catch what he'd thrown before it hit me in my face. It was lava stone, matte black and heavy in my hand. It dangled from a silver chain. Such a simple piece of jewelry.

No way. It couldn't be.

"You've got to be kidding. Why me?" I couldn't begin to understand the blue-eyed monster in front of me, but I obediently slipped the chain over my head, feeling the amulet solid against my chest.

"Over a hundred years ago, two busybody old banshees told me someone would need it. I was to keep it safe even though someone would try to take it from me. *Over and over again.* I underestimated how persistent that someone would be." Gabriel grimaced at the memory. "You know I left Havenwood Falls for a long time. I lost every memory I ever had of this place. Strangely, I never got rid of the amulet. But I'm tired now. It's exhausting, you know, hanging on to secrets for so long. You deal with it now. She's yours."

The dismissal in his voice was clear. And I knew he wasn't just talking about the necklace.

Alina led me out of the room and down a small hallway to a flight of stone stairs that led down, down, and farther still, until we came to a corridor lined entirely in stone from the walls to the ceiling. Even the doors were concrete. She stopped outside of the first door with no window—a solid concrete block on hinges—and paused before grabbing the knob.

"I don't know if she's awake yet, but I'm going to count to three, and when I open the door, you run inside because I'm going to slam it shut as fast as I can. You might have some protection from her being her mate—but she'll kill me with her mind like that. You'll fix her, won't you? You're her mate, right? Gabe said it was different for your kind. Even if you have to take her away, it's okay. Just keep her safe, okay? I love her." Alina's voice broke off on a sob at the end. I thought about giving her a hug to console her, but a wave of nausea took me by surprise at the thought of putting my hand, no matter how chaste, on a woman other than my mate. The vampire upstairs probably wouldn't like it either.

My Hannah was just on the other side of that heavy concrete door. I could smell her scent. I could feel her fear like tiny wings, beating at the air. My beast screamed inside me, clawing frantically at my insides, demanding I get to her immediately. This had better work, or we would both suffer endlessly.

I nodded at Alina, who squared her shoulders, moved her hands over the doorknob, and said a few words I didn't understand. I heard a click, then the door swung open. Alina's hands gave me a shove, and I stumbled through the entrance as the door swung shut behind me. There was a heavy metallic sound as the lock caught, and I was alone in a completely empty room. Empty except for a small form huddled against the floor, the charred and tattered remains of her clothing hanging off her in rags.

There were scorch marks on the walls, the floor, and the ceiling. Like her body had been the epicenter of a rage blast that rocked the room. Not a stick of furniture. Not a table or chair. Just my Hannah, bunched in the corner, her knees pulled up to her chest and head resting on her forearms.

As the door clanged shut and I walked farther into the room, she lifted her head. Her eyes blazed bright orange, amber, and gold. The swirling color of autumns leaves, back-lit by some unholy light. It was her fire. Blazing internally, it glowed from behind her irises, waiting to be released. Again.

Was she in there? My Hannah? My poor, confused mate. Was I too late to fix this? I had to try.

Her head cocked to the side as she watched me, the movement that of a wild animal. A single silvery tear slid from the corner of her eye, down her cheek, and into the curve of her neck. She shifted ever so slightly as I walked closer still. Tense. Tightly wound. Ready to spring. A low keening sound filled the room. A mourning cry.

My heart shattered.

"Oh, baby," I whispered brokenly. "I'm so fucking sorry. Come here. I'm so sorry." I held my arms out helplessly. As she reared back and sprung, her mouth opened wide and liquid heat poured out, blasting across the distance between our two bodies.

Inferno.

CHAPTER 12

HANNAH

*N*ightmares are filthy creatures, trapping you in the web of your own mind, swallowing you whole until you are nothing but a screaming mass of nerves, not knowing what's real and what is fantasy. That's where I was. Trapped in a nightmare of boiling anger. Emotions I couldn't describe ripping and tearing at my flesh from the inside. The madness ate at my mind until I was a seething ball of rage.

I tried to burn it away. I tried to burn it all away, but I still felt the pain. The clawing sense of loss. Abandonment. Complete and utter emptiness. And why? Why did I feel so empty, so incomplete? For the life of me I couldn't remember. Maybe I burned the memory.

Chevy came to me in this dream. I saw him standing in the flame. I know I made him up inside my head. I'd already gone crazy moments before. All the way down I'd slipped. Into the madness. So I burned him up too. He was just a figment of my imagination anyway. I was alone in this room, screaming at the walls, burning away the feelings that just. Kept. Coming.

It hurts. Chevy, help me.

But Chevy couldn't help me. I already turned him into ashes.

But I could still hear his voice, and he just kept talking. Calling me baby. Saying he was sorry.

Sorry for what? He didn't make me crazy. Or maybe he did?

How long had I been locked in this room? Hours? Days? Did I even exist in the passing of time anymore?

I missed him. Missed his hands. Missed that infuriating smile. I missed the way he shoved his shirtsleeves up to his elbows. I liked that a lot. The way most girls liked gray sweatpants. That's how I felt about Chevy's arms.

It was probably the crazy talking, but I made Chevy up inside my head again. This time he was holding me, and his voice was so close, so real. I wanted so badly to believe. So I gave in to the crazy and just for a moment, let myself think he was really there.

"Don't disappear."

I whispered the words, and the voice that had been crooning above me halted. The hand that had been stroking my hair stilled, and the warm arms that were circled around me froze.

"What did you say?" The voice was nothing but a croak. The voice of a man who'd been screaming my name, maybe even crying. Words from a throat so raw they could barely make a sound. How long had he been screaming? Hours? Days?

"Please don't disappear."

I would die if he did. I needed to believe. To open my eyes and see him in front of me. To believe that I wasn't just crazy and making him up again. That Chevy was here in front of me, holding me, touching me. If that was taken away from me, I would crumble into dust and pray to anyone listening that the madness didn't resurrect me again.

"Please be real." And the hands that had been patting my hair gripped my shoulders and brought me in for a bone-crushing hug. His chest was warm. A direct contrast to the cold concrete of the floor beneath me. Everywhere my skin was exposed. What happened to my clothes?

What happened to Chevy's clothes? My vision cleared as the touch of his skin on mine melted the red haze away. The cooling comfort of his presence was a balm to my raw emotions, and the longer I allowed myself to stay there, protected by his embrace, the clearer my mind became.

Maybe I wasn't crazy.

"Where are we?" I threw the question to the wind.

"We're in the dungeon under Gabriel's house."

Ew. "Like a sex dungeon?"

Chevy was silent for a moment, but his hands stayed busy, running up and down my arms and back, making sure I wasn't going anywhere.

"Actually, I think it's more of a dungeon dungeon. There's not shit in here but us. It's a concrete cell."

"What the hell am I doing in a cell?" But as soon as the question left my mouth, the memories flooded my mind. Gabriel. Flames. Chaos. Destruction. "Alina."

I jerked upright, but Chevy's hands held me still.

"Shh." He soothed with his hands and his words. "She's fine. Gabriel's fine."

"I don't care about him." But the sharp pain in my chest said that was a lie.

"You should care. He gave me this." Chevy brought my hand up and pressed it over something on his chest. Something bumpy and organic, covered in holes and attached to a metal chain. I splayed my fingers wide and saw the matte black pendant peeking through the underside of my hand.

"What? I don't understand."

"He gave it to me. To protect me. To save you. Well, he threw it at my head, but I feel like it came from a good place." Chevy laughed brokenly, but I couldn't join him. Sobs caught in my chest, and I swallowed them down hard.

Shit. Uncle Gabe came through in the clutch.

Tears pricked my eyes—of sadness, of relief. Probably both things, but Chevy kissed them all away with the soft touch of his lips to the corners of my eyes. Gentle kisses. Beautiful touch. The mate bond hummed between us, pleased for the first time since Chevy and I had come together. I pressed my hand more firmly over the amulet on Chevy's chest. Felt through it, through the hard stone to the warm flesh underneath. And further still beneath that, to the spirit that lived there, deep within the vessel that was Chevayo Walker. I felt it respond, preening at the recognition.

"Do you accept us?" Chevy felt it. He knew what I was doing.

I choked on my response. "Yes."

"I'll never leave you. I can't, and I won't. So if you aren't ready —" Chevy paused, taking a deep breath and gathering the courage to finish his sentence. "I won't leave you. So if you aren't ready to go with me, I'll stay here with you. I have it on good authority from a witchy tattoo artist that there's nowhere safer when you don't want to be found than Havenwood Falls."

He was so perfect. I didn't deserve him. And there was no way I would make him *figure something out* when the mate issue was so much bigger than the two of us. We may have been the first to experience these things, but there was a whole generation of descendants who needed to know. Needed hope. I would do whatever I needed to do.

But I couldn't find the words.

I turned in his arms and kissed him, hesitant at first until he responded, opening his mouth and pressing more firmly into mine. That was what I wanted. What I needed. This was the last thing. My acceptance of his beast and the joining of our bodies. Right?

Had I thought complete submission was bad? I couldn't remember why, but now all I wanted was for him to take control, to put his hands on me in a less than gentle way, and make me his for real. Not in a teasing, tormenting way. Not in a drunk mate bond lust kind of way. But in a possessive, *keep you forever because I need you and can't live without you* kind of way.

But he never made a move past kissing me back. His arms stayed locked around me, holding me gently, but he made no move to deepen the kiss or touch me any further than he already was.

What gives?

"What are you doing?" Or rather what was he *not* doing?

"What are *you* doing?"

Did he really need an explanation? "Chevy, if you think I'm leaving this room without binding you to me for the rest of our lives, you're nuts. Regardless of whether I leave or you stay, I'm not going through this again. So make me an honest woman and let's get with the sexy."

A huff of laughter vibrated against my back before his booming laughter filled the air and reverberated off the cement walls of the underground cell. He laughed so hard he fell over from his sitting position and landed on his back on the concrete floor. I don't know what he thought was so funny, but he was beautiful lying there, and it wasn't just his chest that was bare. Chevy didn't have a stich of clothes on.

"Why are you naked?"

Chevy grinned and rested his arms behind his head, looking completely at home in an empty stone cell. "You blasted me with everything you had when I came into this room. If it wasn't for the necklace, I would be charcoal dust on the wall right now." He was grinning—the idiot—but my blood ran cold.

I really had tried to turn Chevy to ashes. I hadn't made that up inside my head.

I killed him. With my fire. *I hurt him.*

"You didn't hurt me. I'm right here." I didn't realize I said the words out loud until he responded, and the tears, hot and streaming, flooded my eyes. They spilled so fast, they burned my skin on the way down, cutting hot tracks across my cheeks.

"I've never used my fire to hurt anyone in my life. I almost lost you. I almost killed you."

He kissed me then, for lack of a better way to appease my suffering. A hot kiss, a commanding kiss. And I had no choice but to submit, because we both wanted me to. It was the last thing to ease both of our suffering, and never mind the place—it was the perfect time.

There was no resistance from me as he guided my body over his own, no fight against the raging need. I felt the bond flare up then, radiant. Not like the caustic rage of my fire, but a healing glow. This was good. This was right. Chevy wasn't being aggressive either, which was directly opposite of all the times we'd come together before. Not that I didn't like him in control, because to be honest, that was amazing too. But he wasn't trying to push me, to make me do something I wasn't sure about.

He let me take the lead.

This wasn't a wild mating or two people thrown into a storm of clashing bodies and need. This was beautiful, warm, and pure. Enough to almost make me forget we were on the concrete floor in a burned-out husk of a dungeon cell.

"This is awkward." Chevy smiled, and I saw the corner of his mouth was cracked and bleeding.

"I thought the amulet protected you?"

He looked uncertain for a moment. "Yeah, from the fire, it did. But um, you have a mean right hook, Hannah."

"Oh my god! I punched you?" I ran my hands over his arms and legs as he lay still on the floor, a bemused smile on his face. I was just checking for other injuries, but the swelling under my butt proved he thought otherwise. Laughing, he grabbed my hands and placed his lips across the knuckles of each one.

"Relax Hannah. I'm fine. But you can always kiss it and make it better." He was right. I could.

So I did.

I leaned into him as he half lay, half sat on the concrete floor and ran my tongue delicately over the corner of his mouth, tasting the slight tang of blood as I caressed the cut. He groaned into my mouth. Pain? Or pleasure? Maybe both. The stiffness pressing under my lap confirmed my suspicions. It was both. What a wholly inappropriate place to be taking advantage of Chevy, but take advantage I would. I liked the power of being on top. I was in control—this was my show.

I was brave, and I loved it.

Grabbing both of his hands, I pressed them to my breasts, palm down. The last time he touched me there I'd been bent over my work station and hadn't been able to enjoy it fully. Now I could, and I wanted his hands on me, both of them. He closed them by reflex as his fingers massaged in circles.

"Touch me," I commanded, and he obeyed, opening his mouth wide to accommodate my searching tongue. Yes. This was what I wanted. What I needed. I don't know why I ever ran away from it before. Chevy's body was the medicine I needed to fix the broken things. I welcomed him with open arms.

He pulled away, and I whimpered at the loss but pleasure came screaming back as he moved his mouth away from mine and brought his head to my breasts, leaving a sucking, biting trail across my chest.

The world fell away. There were no walls, no locked room in the basement of the Lilith Nest. There was only me and Chevy, our bodies burning together, strengthening the bond like we should have in the beginning if we only hadn't been so very naïve. But now we knew and we could do better. We could pave the way for the others who didn't know. But before that, we had to become whole ourselves. Had I thought loving a man would make me less of myself? That I would lose that thing that made me Hannah, my power?

I'd been stupid to worry about such trivial things. Stupid to focus on a hundred-year-old necklace that even my great-grandmother didn't give a shit about. I only needed Chevy. He only needed me. He shifted then, lifting me up and shifting position so when he brought me down again, it was to sheathe him fully, gently at first, then my body stretched to accommodate him with more force.

Chevy was already becoming accustomed to my likes and dislikes, and he proved it by lifting me up gently and bringing me down hard, thrusting up as I rocketed down.

More. I wanted more of him. I opened myself fully to accept all of him. Not just the man but the beast as well, into my heart and into my soul. As our bodies joined, mouths and flesh, the mate bond became a liquid thing, pouring over both of our bodies and solidifying like a shield.

"Hannah, do you accept me?" He'd asked me that before, and I'd answered him with words, but this time, I answered with my heart as well. And I knew, as the stars exploded and our bodies flew apart into miniscule pieces, slowly drifting back together to a crumpled heap on the floor, this was it for me.

We would stay in Havenwood Falls for now, strengthening our bond and learning about each other. The issue with Chevy's people —it was bigger than just him and me. This thing we experienced? Mates were their birthright. Who were the elders to take that away? How many people had lived, grown old, and died without ever knowing their other half existed? All for what? Genetics?

Bullshit.

We'd fix it for them. Whatever it took. This was my purpose, and I accepted it wholly.

"Why do you look so fierce?" Chevy said from underneath me. I lay where I'd collapsed on top of him, my head on his chest, listening to his heart beating beneath me.

"I'm just thinking about where we go from here. What do we do now?"

Chevy's fingers combed through my hair, smoothing the strands away from my face. It was strangely soothing. "We'll do the best thing we can to prove the mate bond exists. We'll live."

Such a simple response. How like a man to wrap it up in such a nice package with a pretty bow.

Speaking of package, there was a telltale pressure under my butt, and I could not believe he was that raring to go, especially after the events that had just occurred.

"Are you serious right now?"

"What? I've got my sexy mate on top of me. And you're naked. It would be weird for me not to respond to you."

I raised my head to look at him, and he grinned.

"But we just had sex. And we're in a dungeon."

"But it's a sex dungeon. I mean, if it wasn't before, it is now." His hands were wandering now, and I liked what they were doing. He was right. We had turned this cell into a sex dungeon. It was kind of hot in an *almost killed my mate when I was out of my head but instead we had some sex about it and made up* kind of way.

"But we have to go up sometime." They were waiting for us. I didn't think they would come blasting through the door, but still.

I squealed when Chevy's searching hands moved under my body, then gasped when he found a rhythm with his fingers I couldn't stop from leaning into. Mate sex was no joke. *Would it always be like this?*

He smiled against my mouth. "There is no one in that house upstairs who has the slightest interest in what we're doing down here. We'll go up later."

I started to argue, but forgot what I was going to say when his mouth found mine and he kissed me, hot and deep.

Whatever. We'd go up later.

We hope you enjoyed this story in the Havenwood Falls world featuring a variety of supernatural creatures. Havenwood Falls is a collaborative effort by multiple authors. If you haven't already, be sure to read Great Granny River and Papa Jonas's story in *Kiss the Ashes* by Desiree Lafawn. You can also read Gabe and Alina's story in *Stolen Wishes* by Victoria Flynn.

Books in the Havenwood Falls Sin & Silk series:

Taming the Beast by Nadirah Foxx
Plans Laid Bare by J.D. Nelson
Shift of Fate by Victoria Escobar
Stolen Wishes by Victoria Flynn
Damned Allure by Justine Winter
Savage Salvation by Kristie Cook
Dark Seduction by Michele G. Miller & R.K. Ryals
Soul Laid Bare by J.D. Nelson

Stray With Me by E.J. Fechenda
Chase the Flames by Desiree Lafawn
Flirting With Death by Nadirah Foxx

Also try the signature line, Havenwood Falls, the historical paranormal line, Legends of Havenwood Falls, and stories from the local supernatural college in Sun & Moon Academy.

Stay up to date at www.HavenwoodFalls.com

Subscribe to our reader group and receive free stories and more!

ABOUT THE AUTHOR

Desiree Lafawn is a roller-skating, anime-watching amateur foodie who loves wine and snacks. Especially snacks. She writes contemporary romance, romantic suspense, and paranormal romance in her Northwest Ohio home, where she lives with her husband, two children, and two rowdy cats.

ACKNOWLEDGMENTS

I could not publish a single word of this book without the help of the magnificent Havenwood Falls editing team. That's the truth. To all of the authors who let me borrow your characters to support my story, thank you so much. Victoria Flynn, I love to pick on Gabe, but I can't help it. He's trying so hard to be good for Alina, and Hannah tests his patience so much. He could end her in a second; we all know it. Kristie Cook, thank you for always being available for support, critique, and for that amazing discussion about the direction penises point when they're hard.

Yes, that happened.

Havenwood Falls, I love you so much.

AN EXCERPT

~ A Havenwood Falls Sin & Silk Novella ~

HAVENWOOD FALLS sin & silk

Flirting with Death

SF BENSON WRITING AS

NADIRAH FOXX

Flirting With Death (A Havenwood Falls Sin & Silk Novella) by Nadirah Foxx

What do you do when Death is in love with you?

Monte Tayute, laid-back biker and skilled computer hacker, has been haunted by visions of a gorgeous woman in black. It's an endless dream with the two meeting on a dark road at Samhain. Nothing the nagual shifter tries seems to rid him of the constant image now playing havoc with his life.

In a different realm, Pandora is having her own recurring vision. Hers is of a man who rides a motorcycle on a lonely road. The shinigami—a death spirit of the Japanese underworld—doesn't want hers to stop. On the contrary, Pandora wants to know if the man is real.

When life meets death, the sparks fly. Monte allows Pandora to experience pleasure and love for the first time. Unfortunately, there's an entity who's been waiting on Pandora for over a century, and he's not playing around.

Pandora is supposed to become Death's bride, but Monte isn't ready to give her up.

It all comes down to a game between the shifter and Death. If Monte plays the cards right, he might cheat Death and keep Pandora. Fail, and Death will be the only one happy.

FLIRTING WITH DEATH

BY NADIRAH FOXX

The soft din of humans chattering was a pleasant change from the usual nothingness. I glanced around the dimly lit sushi restaurant, admiring the different colors and expression-filled faces. It was all so different from Yomi-no-kuni—the Japanese shadow realm. The murky netherworld only contained shades of gray.

"What can I get you?" asked a bartender.

I smiled. "Moscato."

My mark was late, but I was good with that. It gave me more time to appreciate earthly things. The server brought my white wine, and I reached for my purse.

"Allow me." The deep voice was unfamiliar.

Hoping it might be my target, I looked up and gasped. The man beside me was larger than life, with hair darker than a raven's feathers and eyes like obsidian. He wore a tailored onyx-colored suit and a matching shirt and tie. If it hadn't been for his wide, too-bright grin, it would have been like staring into darkness. Despite the gloomy exterior, the man was handsome.

He leaned in. "Forgive my interruption. I noticed you were alone."

I batted my eyelashes like an idiot. "Not for long." Before he got the wrong idea, I added, "I'm meeting someone."

His eyebrows arched. "Then I should leave. I wouldn't want your date to jump to any conclusions."

"Not a date. It's a . . ."

I nearly slipped up and told the gorgeous stranger that I was an escort. It was something my kind didn't reveal because of the issues humans had with the concept. They believed that *all* companions were in the business of sex for hire. Well . . . I did get paid and sex sometimes happened, but it wasn't my purpose. I was a shinigami escort—a death spirit who guided souls to the afterlife.

"A what?" the man asked politely.

"It's a business meeting," I replied.

The stranger nodded. "Understood. Perhaps when you're done, we could get to know each other?"

If I were allowed the luxury of a private life, I would entertain the thought. Instead, I opened my bag and removed my business card. I fingered the red embossed torii—a Japanese gate—with my name beneath it. If the man phoned, he'd receive a recorded message saying the number was out of service. I hated the deception, but it wasn't as if I'd see him again. He wasn't the type to be on my list.

"Give me a call." I handed him the white card.

"I'll do that." He pocketed the item, smiled, and said, "You have a great evening, Pandora."

I watched him walk to the exit and then noticed my date. Sadly, it wouldn't be a wonderful night. A bright ethereal glow surrounded the overweight salesman. He was only hours away from death claiming him. This job should be an easy one.

The previous night's target was exhausting. Instead of the traveling salesman giving over to death, he lingered as his soul tried desperately to stay on earth.

His dark eye sockets widen as his diaphanous body shimmers. "Why? I have a wife . . . children . . . They need me."

"Not anymore. It is your time." I wrap my hand around his wrist.

"No!"

I hate stubborn souls. My goal is to entice someone to the afterlife, not drag them. Sometimes, however, I have to resort to darker measures. The flesh suit I regularly wear disintegrates, leaving behind my true skeletal form. My face elongates and sharp, pointed teeth appear as my bluish lips part. I wail like a banshee.

The ear-piercing screech nearly unravels the businessman's spirit as he scurries toward the bright light. When the portal closes, my job is done, and I slink away, reconstructing my corporeal form as I go.

I was made for pleasure, but when needed to, I could scare the shit out of anyone.

Gazing out my apartment window, I tried to put the episode out of my mind, but the colorless realm didn't help. There was nothing in Yomi-no-kuni to please the eye. No division between sky and land. No green grass or flowers to gaze upon. Only shadows and endless phantasms—other death spirits and souls punished for all eternity.

I was frustrated, and the reluctant salesman didn't help. It was supposed to be a two-night engagement—one to get to know him, and the second to escort him into the great beyond. It didn't happen that way. Instead, I only had the one night with him, but Madame Izanami—a.k.a. Madame Death—didn't care as long as the job was done.

In all honesty, shinigami had a better existence than what normal reapers endured. Death's creations didn't hang around anywhere for long or maintain corporeal forms. shinigami did both.

Some called us monsters or creatures of darkness. Not entirely false, but without shinigami, souls would flounder and exist as ghosts. With us, they got a choice—a ghostly existence or a glorious afterlife. Most chose the latter.

Thankfully, the disparaging names didn't bother me. As I drew out a man's last breath, I heard more scintillating ones. Honestly, was it wrong for humans to die with a smile on their faces? I wasn't ashamed of what I did, but lately I'd wanted something else.

Something more than taking all the time. Death spirits were

hard-wired for harvesting. Most of us had no issue with it, but I wasn't like everyone else. I wanted to see what it was like to receive—passion, love, even friendship.

Don't get it twisted. I wasn't some flighty female dying to hop into bed with each and every mark on my list. The night didn't always end up between the sheets. Some men liked talking and having their ego stroked. It was an admirable way of counting down to the end of a life. But then there were the ones who preferred having their dicks stroked instead. Hey, whatever floated their boats —I didn't judge. It got the job done, but it wasn't enough for me anymore.

In two hundred years, I had yet to experience my own gratification. Talk about major dissatisfaction. Not one man aroused me, taking me to the edge of passion and back again.

When I complained, I received reminders that delight was not something afforded to our kind. In a nutshell, we didn't get to love. The emotion supposedly clouded our judgment and kept us from doing our job. I didn't care. I wanted my chance. Just one night of undying (pun intended) passion in a man's arms.

My bellyaching got so bad that the other death spirits filed grievances, and Madame Death had called me to her cold, dark corner office.

Madame's assistant, a handsome shinigami named Toshi, rakes his black eyes over me and offers a toothy smile. "When you're done with her, how about you and me go out tonight?"

"Not in a million years," I say, and push open the door.

A blast of frigid air hits me, and my form flickers, losing its cohesiveness. The mist, full of despair, parts, and the figure of a woman emerges. Madame is more of a shade than the embodiment of an entity. The gossips claim that the goddess is only a corpse with rotting flesh and maggots crawling in and out of her orifices. Not something I want to view, whether it's true or not.

"Takara, do you know why you're here?"

Madame only uses my given name when I'm in trouble. Realizing the seriousness of the summons, I keep quiet.

"Sit down," she orders.

After I'm seated, she continues, "I'm giving you a chance to explain yourself. I've listened to numerous allegations, and I'm not pleased. Why the constant complaints? This sort of thing isn't like you."

Averting my eyes, I say, "Ma'am, I'm sorry. It's nothing. I just had a bad night."

Although I can't see her stare, I feel its frostiness. She exhales. "Takara, you are one of my best creations. It pains me to see you so disillusioned. Our lot in this world is to guide souls to their final resting place. Love isn't in the equation."

"I know," I say meekly.

"Do you?" Her fingers tap an unseen surface—the only noise in the void—as if my employer is considering her words. "It sets a bad precedent when those at the top of the heap start whining. Continue to do so, and I'll be forced to take you off active duty."

My gaze whips up. "A desk job would kill me."

"A bit of an exaggeration, don't you think? I'd rather confine you than have you bring down morale."

A suspension is much better than the alternative—the worst fate for shinigami. With one snap of Madame's fingers, I could become one of the shadows attached to Yomi-no-kuni.

"Then stop the griping, Takara. We have one job, and one job only. Personal satisfaction comes with successfully completing a task."

"Understood," I say with more conviction than I feel.

"I hope so. I'd rather give out rewards than punishments any day."

That was a week ago. Since then I'd been on my best behavior. I kept my thoughts focused, and when I got bored, I took on extra assignments. It worked for seven agonizingly long days and then it stopped.

My Rattler social media feed pinged on my phone. I turned my attention to the flat-screen television on the wall. DNN—the Death News Network—displayed yet another fatal car crash. The channel was how death spirits got the news of human expirations. Unfortunately, DNN and Rattler were permanent fixtures. You couldn't turn them off, but I could mute the TV. My black stilettos clicked across the floor as I headed to the coffee table in search of the remote.

Before I reached it, the doorbell rang. Odd. I wasn't expecting anyone, and my roommate was out for the evening.

I glanced at my appearance in the full-length mirror. Fortunately, head-to-toe black leather was enjoyed by a lot of the humans I was set up with. I fluffed my ebony-colored hair, applied another coat of Deadly Decay lipstick in Drop Dead Red, and drew in a breath before opening the door.

The handsome stranger from the restaurant was on the other side. How was that possible?

"May I come in, Takara?"

I was too stunned to refuse. *How did he know my given name?*

He was so tall that he had to duck to clear the doorway. Once inside, he went to the sofa and made himself comfortable as if it were a normal thing for him to visit me.

Standing with my hand on the knob, I asked, "How are you here? *What* are you?"

"Death, of course." He spread his long arms over the back of my sofa and crossed his ankle over a knee. "I thought it time we officially met."

Normally, death spirits could sense other supernaturals. But forces, like Death, had a way of screwing with our radar so that we didn't discern them. But why was he there?

Still confused, I joined him in the living room but kept my distance. "And why is that?"

He sighed. "It's customary for a bride-to-be to meet her groom."

My mouth fell open.

Ignoring my silence, Death continued, "It's amazing how your mood has changed since our first meeting. Not important, though. I thought we'd start with dinner on Samhain. We can dine here, or I can take you someplace special."

Dinner with Death?

Was he fucking kidding me?

It was true that I wanted something more, but not with a chaotic entity.

"Takara, is there something wrong?" His dark, lust-filled gaze raked over me, and suddenly I felt naked. "Come sit down. I'd like to get to know you better."

He needed to stop saying that. It wasn't happening.

Thankfully, the door opened behind me. Turning around, I saw Hope—my roommate and created twin. Madame gave us the same waist-length black wavy hair, too-pale skin, and curvy figure. Shinigami are supposed to work in pairs, and she was my designated partner. Sometimes, like the night with the salesman, we got to work alone.

The only obvious difference between Hope and me were our almond-shaped eyes. Mine were deep green while hers were cerulean blue, earning us our listing in the home office's database as Emerald and Sapphire. In the human world, we had supernatural contacts who trolled the various dating services searching for possible marks. If someone said they were into twins or loved green or blue eyes, we were messaged.

"Who's this?" she asked.

"Hope, meet Death."

Her jaw dropped, mimicking my earlier expression.

He pushed to his large feet and walked toward us. "It's a pleasure to meet you, Hope." He placed his enormous hand on my shoulder. "I'll leave now, but will expect you for dinner on Samhain."

I shook my head. "I'm sorry, but I'll have to decline."

Death squeezed, and pain shot through my body, threatening to unravel my corporeal form. "Not an option. Nobody turns me down."

I swallowed hard. Hope's worried gaze landed on me.

He eased up his grip and dropped his hand. "Something you should know about me, Takara. When I want something—or someone—I get it. You were promised to me. You shall fulfill your obligation. Don't cross me. I assure you that my punishment would be worse than anything Izanami could do to you."

He stalked toward the door.

After it closed, Hope asked, "What the fuck was that about? What did he mean by you're promised to him?"

"I don't know, but I don't plan on sticking around to find out." Reluctantly, I told her what Death told me.

"If you're supposed to marry an entity—"

"I won't do it. There are other things I want to do."

The man I had been dreaming of for years came to mind. He was tall, mysterious, and rode a motorcycle. If I was about to be shackled for all eternity to Death, maybe it was time to see if the man was real.

Purchase *Flirting With Death* where books are sold.